THE BAD CIRCLE

THE BAD CIRCLE

John Newton Chance

Chivers Press • G.K. Hall & Co.
Bath, England   Thorndike, Maine USA

This Large Print edition is published by Chivers Press, England, and by G.K. Hall & Co., USA.

Published in 1999 in the U.K. by arrangement with Robert Hale Ltd.

Published in 1999 in the U.S. by arrangement with Robert Hale Ltd.

U.K. Hardcover ISBN 0–7540–3547–6 (Chivers Large Print)
U.K. Softcover ISBN 0–7540–3548–4 (Camden Large Print)
U.S. Softcover ISBN 0–7838–0361–3 (Nightingale Series Edition)

The text of this Large Print edition is unabridged.
Other aspects of the book may vary from the original edition.

Set in 16 pt. New Times Roman.

Printed in Great Britain on acid-free paper.

British Library Cataloguing in Publication Data available

Library of Congress Cataloging-in-Publication Data

Chance, John Newton.
    The bad circle / by John Newton Chance.
        p.   cm.
    ISBN 0–7838–0361–3 (lg. print : sc : alk. paper)
    1. Large type books.   I. Title.
[PR6005.H28B34   1999]
823'.912—dc21   98-33776

CHAPTER ONE

1

There are parts of Kent which still escape the dreadful nappy-rash of modern development, and the country around Cob Weary is one such part. The Weary is pronounced Wary as if the ghosts of forefathers wait on lookout to repel the modern touch. There it is possible to feel men are still about to maintain the feud of centuries between those who offered Caesar the olive branch and those who wanted to stick it up his nose.

I was glad to have light thoughts on that still, overcast November afternoon. The house of Cob Weary was as fine a piece of half-timbered, bulging, cultural neglect as one might find in Vandalsland. It fattened in the company of a lost-looking oast house and a huge tithe barn which looked as if spiritual wish was still holding it up. The neglect made me angry before I ever met Arethusa Greco-Browne.

('Arethusa?' I told my partner. 'It can't be. They only have that name for battleships'— 'Right,' he said.)

I left my car and approached the front porch with apprehension, because the upper storey leaned forward as if choosing a right moment to fall on me.

Before I could knock at the oak door it was opened by a pretty woman in medieval fancy dress with low bodice that pushed her bosom up and almost out of cover like a pair of animated melons. She wore a mob cap with a black bow in front and a full skirt below which her black-slippered feet 'like little mice stole in and out' to cadge a phrase.

'You are Mr Keyes,' she said, smiling, 'and Mrs Greco-Browne is waiting for you.'

That the great lady was waiting for me, instead of expecting me put me in the wrong to start with. I am a sensitive man when it comes to feeling guilty about nothing.

At places inside the building it was necessary to duck my head for fear of brain damage but we came into a large room, wherein, it looked to me as if everybody ate, dressed, scrubbed, plucked birds, whittled wood, repaired clocks, read hundreds of books to their middles and then dropped them face down—or bookmarked them with unopened official letters—and drank from many bottles while playing the Tarot cards.

Everywhere it was a scene of something attempted, nothing done.

There was a large space in front of a huge fire-place which was covered by a woolly mat, thick as grass, on which a woman stood, feet apart, her back to the half-forgotten log fire in the vast grate.

2

The woman was almost six feet tall and wore riding breeches, brown leather leggings and boots and an open-necked white shirt which stood as far out as a ship's figurehead. She had black hair scragged back to an untidy back bun and wore black-rimmed spectacles which made her blue eyes look specially keen.

She looked at me, then putting two fingers to her front teeth, blew a sharp, ear piercing whistle. As if by magic, five large dogs, two English Setters, two Irish and a Golden Retriever, appeared from chairs, a sofa, piles of clothes on the floor. They stretched, shook their heads and sometimes the whole lot, tails as well, so the air became thick with loose hairs, and then rushed out through an open door and vanished, barking happily, into the distance.

She looked at me while the woman in the cap stood by.

'You are Mr Keyes, and you have something for me,' said the woman by the fire. 'I am Arethusa Greco-Browne and I claim the document you have brought in your briefcase.'

'Of course,' I said, until then not having had the chance to speak. 'It will take you some time to go through, so I have booked a room at the inn for tonight to give you plenty of time.'

I tried to put my case on the huge table so as to open it. Seeing my difficulty, the woman in the cap swept the entire works of a clock off the table with her arm and smiled at me.

3

'Rubbish,' said Arethusa Greco-Browne arrogantly. 'You will have a room here to sleep and Anna will keep you warm.'

'I was a call girl until I slipped a disc with an Australian athlete,' Anna explained as if describing her stay at a convent. 'It's all right now.'

'I got hold of her bloody back and jerked it,' said Arethusa Greco-Browne, making savage gestures with her hands. 'Right back into position. You might wonder what she is doing, dolled up like that. It is because she feels she was born out of her proper time and always dresses like that on Thursdays. Give me the document, Mr Keyes.' She held out her hand.

I took the document and walked round the table, tripping twice on articles of discarded clothing. She took the parchment, her eyes steadily on me.

'I dress like this when I feel I want to beat people,' she said. 'It makes me feel I can.' She began to read the heavy script.

By that time I realized that the suspicions voiced to me that Arethusa might be off-balance were probably true. But people can be barmy intermittently, and the scene presented by the two women brought to my mind a remark by a psychiatrist long ago:

'Some people get pressured by odd desires, but they find that by dressing up they can get rid of it.'

Looking at the big woman I thought it quite

4

likely that she felt she would like to beat somebody with some instrument, but that, having dressed like a hunting butcher, she might get rid of the desire very quickly.

I felt apprehension, but I had been told to expect, at least, alarm, and at the most, a need to get out quick. But what filled me with dismay was the prospect of staying in this overstuffed barnyard. A refined glutton, such as myself, is turned sick at the thought of food mixed up with dog hairs and yesterday's egg on the beef plate.

'Tell Harry to clean out the guest room,' said Mrs Browne, without looking up. 'Whereunder heretofore thereafter aforesaid— They get these bits out of old documents and stick them all together like trains in a goods yard,' she cried, and threw the precious document into an empty chair. 'Sod the lot of 'em.'

Anna had gone to an open door behind a chair and suddenly she bawled out, 'Harry!' Come here, yer bugger!'

'Anna!' Mrs Browne shouted. 'Mind your language. I've told you before.'

Anna appeared round the chair.

'I do not understand you. You are all nuts. Big nuts. Coconuts. You tell me to learn English, but when I say what they say you say it is wrong.'

'Don't copy hooligans.'

A large young man with a bronzed chest

which appeared through his torn shirt came through the door and leaned on the back of the chair, looking at Mrs Browne.

'Wot?' he said, and his dark eyes drifted round to me.

'Clean up the guest room.'

He said nothing, but just disappeared, the last vestige seen of him being two fingers held up as a signal of his pleasure in the task given.

Mrs Browne began talking about her late husband, the cause of the documents. He had died rich but tangled, and the lawyers were trying to untangle, but were not quite sure Mrs Browne was the only interested party.

There was a niece, but she had not been seen since coming to stay with Mrs Browne some time before I arrived.

('Keep an eye open for her, or for what's happened to her. It could be interesting,' my partner had said.)

Which was why, I, a detective by trade, had been sent with the documents instead of a lawyer.

Anna came back into the room. Her mistress looked at her.

'I feel better,' Mrs Browne said. 'I'll change.' And she started to take her shirt off.

I glanced at the workless clock. Anna started looking round the floor, kicking heaps of clothing, and bringing pieces of apparel out of chairs then dropping them back.

'Which was you wearing?' she said.

'Never mind that,' said the big woman throwing herself into a chair. 'Get these bloody boots and things off and then I'll have the grey costume. Perhaps Mr Keyes would like tea?' she added, looking at me.

'Don't bother about me,' I said quickly. I had to glance at her to speak. With her leg up and struggling with Anna for a boot, it seemed that the resources of the black lace bra were being wobbled into near disaster.

I picked up a book or two and glanced at the pages but the strain of not looking at the struggling strip made it impossible to concentrate elsewhere.

Then there was a sudden thumping, crashing, roaring and droning from overhead. It sounded as if an aircraft had hit the roof.

'It's Harry, beating the carpet with the vacuum cleaner,' said Mrs Browne. 'He dislikes doing what he calls maid's work.'

They had got the boots and leggings off and Mrs Browne stood up and pulled her belly in to unfasten the breeches.

'I never saw my husband for the last twenty-three years,' she said. 'I left him when I was twenty-four. He was a thoroughly bad old lot, I'm afraid.'

And so was she, I had heard in my briefing, for Cob Weary had been the property of an old man who had pushed his old wife over a cliff at Margate because of his lust for Arethusa.

'She weren't no good. She were barren,' he

explained, when asked at court why he had chosen the Golden Wedding to murder his wife. He had been found of unsound mind, and yet there had been no one to oppose the transfer of the deeds of Cob Weary to Arethusa Greco-Browne.

Some of the details of The Taking of Cob Weary were comic on the surface, pathetic just below, and dead sinister at bottom.

And on top of various suspect events in the past there was the fact that Lauren Hazel had recently visited her aunt, and there was the known end of her activities. Whether she had left or was still there was a matter for guess or hope, depending which way one was affected.

The lawyers were thinking the worst, but on first sight it was almost possible the girl had got lost in the mess which Cob Weary had become.

But there was an interest she could claim in the tangled estate of the late Greco-Browne, so the lawyers believed.

They also believed that Arethusa knew of the claim the girl might have to set against her own. And if the claim could show that the girl was, in fact, Greco-Browne's daughter by Arethusa's sister, then there would surely be a lot of sparks to fly.

And that is what the lawyers did think, and that was why the long and confusing, heavily detailed 'sorting-out' of the estate had been brought by me.

'There!' said Arethusa and stood up newly

arrayed in frayed slacks and a sweater that fitted her bust like a coat of paint.

The uproar from above was continued. The place looked and sounded like a madhouse, which was probably the effect I was meant to get.

But the real effect on me was far from what she had intended. The posing and noisy assertion lacked an outward expression of a sinister inside. Had I been a girl going into that house and met with the same exhibition I would have been badly frightened.

There was great strength, a barely hidden arrogance about the posturings of the big woman and the amused, ironic servitude shown by the woman, Anna. The thunderous rebellion from upstairs seemed to be directed more at me than my hostess.

2

'He can start down here when he's finished,' Mrs Browne said, staring round. 'The place looks like an abandoned brothel in a cattle market. Why doesn't Mrs Wicks come every day?'

'She said she'll not come again last week,' said Anna. 'Then you told her to go jump in the pond and she said—'

Arethusa held up a hand. 'I remember what she said, and what I did. Shut up. I had just forgotten for the moment. Clear a chair. Mr

Keyes hasn't sat down yet, thanks to the slovenly way you run this place. And don't argue. Clear that chair!'

'That one?' protested Anna, defiantly. 'But that's where—'

Before she could reveal the horror that had been done in that chair, Mrs Browne pointed at her and went a step nearer to her.

'I'll—kill—you—Anna!' she said. 'Go and get the bags!'

'What bags are these you say?'

'Mr Keyes's bags. In his car!'

'No, they're not as a matter of fact,' I said, jumping desperately into the unexpected opening. 'I left them at the inn where I booked.'

Mrs Browne turned to me, and at the same moment, the din upstairs stopped as if from awe of her wrath which looked about to be fired in my direction.

But from somewhere upstairs, Harry shouted and she stopped and looked up to the beamed ceiling.

'What's the matter with you, Harry?' she called.

There was no answer except the sound of Harry's hobnailed boots crashing down some distant staircase. A second or two later he came into the room and pointed right into the dragon's face.

'You sent me up there!' he shouted. 'You sent me up there and you knew bloody well

10

what was up there! I ain't going in there any more, missus! That's your affair, what's up there. I'm no more going in that room, I tell you, no matter what! You must be mad sending me up there. What did you think I'd do? Faint? You can do what you want with it. It's yours, that is! That's your problem, missus. Don't you try and mess me up in it!'

He turned to walk out. The woman was white but whether from rage or from the sudden alarm at having some secret discovered I couldn't tell.

'You needn't bother any more!' she said. 'Mr Keyes is staying at the inn.'

A sigh of relief almost escaped from me.

It was dusk outside then and the vivid squalor of the big room began to soften. It did not soften the look on Mrs Browne's face as she glared after the departing Harry. She controlled her anger as she turned to me.

'Look in about nine tonight,' she said. 'I may have had time to go through the document by then. Thank you, Mr Keyes. You have been most patient!'

Anna took my arm to show me out. I picked up my briefcase from the table as Mrs Browne marched out of the room in the direction Harry had gone.

'She will hit him,' said Anna, with a regretful sigh. 'Then he will hit her. They like to hit each other. It is rude really—You walk so fast, Mr Keyes!'

I was walking fast without noticing it in my keenness to go. At the door Anna smiled again.

'I see you at nine o'clock?'

'Yes, Anna. You see me at nine o'clock.'

I got into the car before I realized that I was frightened. The atmosphere in the house was indescribable. I was almost terrified at the thought of what Harry had found up in the guest room. A body? The decomposing body of the missing girl?

I drove off quickly as if to get away from my own imaginings.

*   *   *

The inn was small and clean and full of telephones. Telephones were the innkeeper's hobby. He made a publicity feature of it. A phone in each bedroom, behind the bars, in the hall, in the kitchen and even in the upstairs bathroom. He was eager to explain how easy it was to phone from his establishment no matter what you happened to be doing.

He saw my car out of the open door. He was a keen spotter of car numbers, also.

'I saw that earlier on,' he said. 'Outside the Dame of Doom's it was. Have you called on the Hag? Another two like her and you'd have 'em all round the old stewpot boiling up sailors' thumbs and all that caper. Kids won't pass Cob when 'tis getting dark.' He laughed.

He showed me into a small bedroom and left me. I threw my bag on the bed. I lifted the phone and he answered me from downstairs.

'I'll give you the outside line,' he said, and the dialling started to buzz. I dialled my office and got my second partner, Leslie.

I think the first thing I said was, 'I don't like this. It's like stirring up a cesspit. A witches' pool.'

'Elbow left a message for you if you rang,' Leslie said. 'He said you needn't hang on if you don't like the look of it. The lawyers have got the shakes about it now. Second thoughts have wobbled their greying knees.'

'They want me to pull out?'

'They don't want you to get into trouble if it would pull them into the same,' he said. 'On the other hand, they say, if you think you can handle it diplomatically—and so on. It's up to you.'

'I've left the document with her. I'm supposed to get her to sign it, aren't I? What's frightened them?'

'That's what we would like to know, but they say it's just prudence, professional prudence; that is, professional wind-up. I had a word with the clerk and he nudged that it was possible multiple murders had gone on down there and it wouldn't be nice if their client had done them.' He laughed.

'Laugh on, but the whole atmosphere of the place brought to mind decomposing bodies hidden in the cupboards. I said I'd go back there tonight. I'm staying in the pub.' I gave him the number. 'Is anything known about this woman?'

'You mean a nasty anything? All I've heard is she got the old man to shove his missus off the cliff. Have you seen the girl there?'

'No. But I was there for only an hour. She could have been somewhere around.'

'Under the floorboards?'

'Cut that out. It isn't so funny when you get into the damn place, Leslie. It's very easy to imagine that sort of thing.'

'Are you sure it's not you? It seemed a bit lurid to me when I first heard it, so perhaps it played on your expectations.'

'Could be. I'll ring tomorrow.'

I sat on the bed and tried to sort out just what I did think about Cob Weary, and how much of it was nervous reaction jerking like a touch on a mouse's whiskers.

I wondered what Harry *had* found in the dreaded guest room. I wondered why the lawyers, having devised the plan of my taking the document, in order to see the inside of what was going on at Cob, had suddenly got cold feet. What had they suddenly found out? Shouldn't I know what it was? Why hadn't they told us? When had they found it out? Only today?

And then I asked myself the most important question of all.

Should I go back to that place at nine o'clock? Why had she wanted me to go that night?

I got up because a new sort of question came into my mind, which was, 'What the hell's the matter with me, getting frightened like this? Was she really a witch who had got her finger on my nervous system? What rubbish!'

I went down to the bar which was then just open and thought about food over a drink. The landlord was chatty. He started on Cob again, but there was not much that was startling until he mentioned visitors.

'They come and go so fast you don't see 'em go. She scares 'em off with a glare of her basilisk eye, is what some say. I reckon they don't go. She does 'em in and uses 'em for fertilizer. She's mean and very economical.'

'She has had a lot of visitors? You mean she doesn't any more?'

'Used 'em all up!' he said cheerfully, and then became serious. 'I'm joking, of course. But she's a bloody queer woman, all the same. *And* the Alsatian—though I wouldn't mind that on a cold night.'

'Alsatian?'

'The maid or whatever she may be down there. That's where she came from; Alsatia. Half French, half German and half hairy dog. I can't see her doing a maid's work, somehow. And then there's Harry. Well he can be useful

15

and he can work when he feels like it. The only thing is he's nicknamed the Stallion round here, but it's not for me to criticize a man's way of making his living bright and smiling. He's not a bad fellow unless he gets wild, then he can be very bad. I would reckon, meself, he's the innocent of the three of 'em.'

He refilled my glass.

'Mark you, there's a lot of bad said about 'em—or her I should say, because of the old man that used to have it. They was always an affectionate pair, the old man and maid, and it's reckoned the woman somehow *made* him push his missus off the cliff. Some sort of evil eye stuff. You can't blame people for making things up like that. And she encourages it?'

'Mrs Browne?'

'Oh yes. The more they say about her that's bloody wicked the more she laughs at 'em. She's a right weird one. A show-off really. When something's strange or out of the common, people always lick on to something evil. They never seem to think a geezer might be shy, or awkward, or got a bit of a twist. It always has to be he's nasty, or dangerous.'

'You prefer to give a man a chance first?'

'A man's all right with me till he can't pay for the beer I let him have on tick. That's when my view changes.'

I ordered some food and he went off to instruct his wife.

Mrs Browne, the Alsatian, Harry. None in

16

the three appeared to be underdog. As if they formed a small tight circle held together because each one knew enough about the other two to hold position in the ring.

A Bad Circle. But what was in the middle of the defensive ring? Was it an evil thing? Or were my fears of evil a wrong reaction to the horrors of the inside of tumbledown Cob?

CHAPTER TWO

1

I went back to Cob at nine that night. After the talk with my office I had it firmly in my mind to make this last call, as promised to Mrs Browne, and to go back to London first thing in the morning.

Everyone else concerned in the affair was losing their nerve and that unpleasant sensation of funk was spreading to me. I did not like Cob or its inmates, and if there was any unpleasantness to be uncovered there, I would sooner somebody else did it.

When I got there the front door of the tumble-down house was wide open and inside lights shone from the main room on the right of the entrance room.

I banged with the knocker ring and the powerful voice of Mrs Browne answered from the direction of the lights.

'Come in, Mr Keyes.'

I went down into the big room. There are advertisements on television where a dusty, cobwebbed, muddy mansion is miraculously transformed into shining elegance by one application of a spray polish. It seemed that something of the sort had happened in the big room. Either that or all the clutter and such had been shoved underneath, rather than on top of, the chairs and table.

Arethusa Greco-Browne then, with black evening dress and dangling earrings, had a most handsome appearance, as if she, too, had been given the gloss-over with the furniture spray.

She was seated at the shining table between tall candlesticks and seemed to have been in the process of studying the document I had brought.

'Sit down, Mr Keyes.' She indicated a chair at the top of the table, opposite her and about fourteen feet away along the refectory plateau.

'The staff has a night off,' she said, as if it didn't matter but was intended just to stop me nosing around.

She sat back and looked hard at me.

'What is your interest in my niece?' she said.

I was, as she intended, taken aback, and tried not to show it.

'Your niece?' I said, looking blank. 'I have never met her.'

'I know that,' she said. 'I asked what was your interest in her.'

'None,' I said.

She looked down at the document.

'I shall have to see the lawyers about this. It seems to me a tangle.'

'I understand it was a tangle and is not yet quite sorted out, but those are the proposals for assembling certain assets, but this can't be done without your written agreement.'

She was silent for a while. It seemed to me that she didn't like the proposals because they tied everything up too much and she would sooner have the entire leavings of the late Greco-Browne in her hands.

As if she would take flight as soon as she had it.

Why that idea came I don't know, but it was something to do with the fact I felt she would get out of Cob Weary just as soon as she had the money to do it.

She pointed across the room.

'Pour some whisky,' she said. 'It is on the table there.'

I got up, went into a corner where there were a number of bottles of various drinks with a siphon and glasses, which gleamed as if they had also been treated to some instant crystal spray.

When I had got the drinks she flipped through the pages of the document in a restless sort of way, then looked up to take a glass from my hand.

'I shall need more time to think about this,' she said.

I said, 'As I understand it, your signature to the various orders is needed as so much of this fortune is lodged abroad and in special bonds which need authority.'

'But it's recommended that most of it should stay where it is!' she said, angrily. 'And I am not interested in investment. I prefer to choose my own means to do what I want to do, not what is recommended to me.'

'Yes, I can understand that,' I said. 'The lawyers, of course, always look at the long-term benefits.'

'Or this is not a genuine recommendation,' she said, tapping the pages with a finger.

'Not genuine?' I said, surprised that she had seen through it so easily.

'It seems to be like a stalling device.'

'To what ends?' I said, as if I didn't know.

'To keep me from having control of the estate until you find out something which you feel you should know.'

I sat down again and looked at her along the table.

'What possible purpose could that have?' I said.

'There may be some suggestion that I am not the true widow of Greco-Browne.'

I laughed very shortly.

'But surely there's no doubt of that!'

She shrugged.

'People have a habit of not trusting me,' she said.

I wondered just how we were going to handle this woman, when she seemed to see through our intentions and suspicions with such intuitive ease.

'I'm sure it's not that in this case,' I said. 'But you know what lawyers are; so keen on searching for loopholes they cannot see they're always looking through the biggest one.'

'The law itself,' she added. 'Yes.' She looked into the glowing logs of the fire, then took a man-sized swig at her Scotch-and-soda. 'I don't like the way they're doing this. I think I shall go up and see them myself.'

'Will you take the document with you?' I said, hopefully.

'Of course.' She got up and walked to the fire, tall and commanding in the long black dress. 'I suppose you are still wondering what Harry found in the guest room that he made such a fuss about.' She turned and smiled.

'A dead cat?' I said.

'A human cadaver,' she corrected as if that was even less important than a cat.

'A dead body?' I said, hardly able to believe she had said such a thing.

'Yes. Harry hates them. They frighten him. He has a certain simple innocence which is amusing to shock.'

'Do you leave dead bodies for him to find?'

21

'There are a great many here,' she said. 'They were once hidden all over the house and we often find them.'

'You must be joking,' I said. I was genuinely alarmed.

'No,' she said calmly. 'It was a long time ago, of course, and difficult to tell how long, but I'd say more than a century. There really was a doctor of the Frankenstein leaning living here. An experimental fanatic for human creation by his own methods. He bought bodies, he bought skeletons, he bought people. Living people. Even today, people who will sell themselves to provide for someone else may not be easy to find, but they can be found. Such poor wretches were murdered by him—in painless conditions, I hope—and embalmed and kept for future use. It was bodies like that we have found.'

'What do you do about it?' I said, very quietly.

'Nothing. What good does it do to report these things? Nobody knows who they were and if they weren't missed over a century ago they are not likely to be now.

'Besides, you know perfectly well what would happen if it was reported. We should be inundated with police and officials who would probably tear the place apart just for the fun of finding some more. Sentiment should not go as far as to destroy the sentimentalist.'

I wondered that she knew anything about

the sentimental. I was aghast at the idea of living unconcerned in a place where embalmed corpses were likely to fall out of the walls at any time.

That three people could live in this place and only one complain—and that about having to clear it up—was incomprehensible.

'Of course, you are slightly startled,' she said coolly, 'but if you go into the College of Surgeons you will see the stuffed body of Jeremy Bentham sitting in his case staring at you. What's the difference? They're all dead. They are no longer of consequence.'

Well, of course they are of no consequence, but they do seem to mean living beings in a disjointed sort of way to those of us who remain, and there is an innate horror of the charnel house in most normal persons.

Arethusa Greco-Browne was anything but normal, but all the same it is difficult for a normal person with the usual allergies to understand a woman of the sort she seemed to be.

Then I ceased to cower.

'Many thanks for the offer of that room for the night,' I said.

'I'd forgotten anything was wrong up there,' she said. 'And in any case, Harry should have cleared it up without making a fuss.'

'What was I expected to do if I'd found it in my bedroom?'

'You have the choice of fainting or you could have left it out with your shoes.'

23

I stared in astonishment at this wit.

'The best thing I can think is that you're slightly mad,' I said.

'On the contrary, Mr Keyes, I am one of the few sane people. I feel nothing for things that have ceased to exist except in the form of fertilizer for the life of the future.'

'There is pity,' I said.

'Can pity last a hundred years?'

'It does.'

'It is only rekindled by tales of what was and probably was not, a hundred years before. The bogus art of the tear jerker.'

We were silent for a moment.

'What have you done with—those discovered already?'

'Given them a decent burial. I am not entirely pagan.'

'Do you mean a funeral service of some kind?'

'Heavens, no! It is not a question as to whether they must be committed to God or the Devil. They have been chosen a hundred years ago and gone. That's why they don't matter, Mr Keyes. I am surprised you can't see that.'

I drank my Scotch, and then poured another. I was shaken by this whole horror, though what she said was perfectly logical if one only had the mind to think of it that way.

Of course she was right in saying they had gone so long that human concern was no longer a matter for consideration.

Of course she was right not to want her house pulled down because of the evil of a man dead almost as long as his victims.

But there was a point in which she might be even more right, if she had cared to mention it.

It was that, with all these perfectly right burials going on from time to time a more recent body might join in without anybody taking any notice.

Then came another of those shocks which she seemed to be able to deliver right to the heart and the brain at the same time.

'If you are thinking of my niece, Mr Keyes,' she said, with a smile, 'she is at present in Greece.'

I thought it time I went back to the inn. I felt that if I stayed much longer talking casually about such horrors I might either go slightly mad, or perhaps begin to be bent in my outlook and start agreeing with her butcher's view of the physical world.

And I might begin to believe that she really could read what I was thinking at any given time.

2

I went back to London next morning and went into my office that afternoon after a light lunch of a dozen oysters, smoked salmon and Stilton, which went down to justifiable expenses in view of the wear and tear on my nerves after a day with Arethusa Greco-Browne.

Our senior partner's office is a showpiece for the nervously insecure client; a fine Victorian plush, red leather and mahogany room with plenty of velvet and a gold-plated telephone set which would have fitted in Maxim's in 1900. Our partner—we called him Elbow for short as his office cabinet was replenished with three bottles of Harvey's Bristol Cream every day—was a good listener and sounding board.

I went in and told him about the ménage Greco-Browne. He woke up about half way through.

'Are you serious?' he said.

'Dead serious,' I said, and meant it.

'But did *you* see any dead bodies?' he said, curiously.

'I didn't wait.'

'You're too finicky, Keyes my boy. If you'd seen one you could have called in the police and solved the problem.'

'I understood the solicitors weren't keen on that for reasons to do with their proposals.'

'That's true, but if she is a bloody Borgia, one doesn't want to let her go on giving dinner parties and burying the left-overs.'

'Well, that's up to you.'

'It's up to whether you saw any evidence that she wasn't spinning a yarn.'

'No. The man kicked up hell, that's all, but I didn't see why.'

'You say she's coming up to see the lawyers, but the fact is they were her husband's advisers not hers. They don't trust her, as we well know, so how she'll get on with them I don't know.'

'I shudder to think. However, that's their misfortune. What do you suggest we should do about it?'

'Await instructions,' he said with confidence. 'When they've seen her they might have something fresh to say.'

'We shouldn't be waiting long. She said she'd be up today, and she looks to me the sort of woman who says and does in the style of the old one-two. No pause. Well, I'm off for a bath and a rest. The man at the inn is fond of telephones. They go tink-tink all the ruddy night like The Anvil Chorus. He said he thought they were picking up the traffic lights at the junction of the main road.'

I went home. I have an elegant mews cottage behind Park Lane. My wife is wealthy and likes places behind Park Lane. She was away at the time of the Greco-Browne affair. She and one of her sisters had gone over to Ohio to see some friends in Cleveland who were in London and my wife was waiting in Cleveland for them to get back. My wife is careless over making arrangements.

I went into my empty house, made tea, had a bath then sat down and tried to think clearly about Arethusa Greco-Browne.

The story she had told about the lunatic doctor might have been true up to a point, for every now and again there is a mass murderer that turns up in police archives, and every now and again, but more rarely I always hope, such a one doesn't turn up in the police records, but becomes well known as a ghost, like Jack the Ripper. Others don't even appear as ghosts but stay entirely undetected. Their victims are always people who won't be missed for one reason and another.

But she had spoken to me about it openly, as if the weird story was well known locally.

Naturally the tale of death was in the front of my mind because it was so bloody, but it had, in fact, nothing to do with the lady herself and her niece, who was in Greece.

The November afternoon was getting misty with the dusk, and I lit a fire and settled down to a quiet evening, which, with me, is usually a signal for the roof to fall in or some other disruption to strike.

At about a quarter past five there was a knocking at the door and the bell rang twice just to make sure I should not think the knocking was accidental.

I opened the door to a woman in a rich fur cape and wearing a round fur hat.

'Allo, *mon bold capitaine,*' she said, and marched in with the cape swinging splendidly behind her.

'Anna!' I said. 'What on earth are you doing

28

here?' I was about to say 'in your mistress's clothes' but did not, of course.

She stopped by the fire and posed in the cape.

'You like my coat?' she said. 'It is a wages of sin, you know. Not bad pay, you think, perhaps?'

'I wouldn't be so rude. Sit down. What do you want?'

'I do not want another fur coat,' she said. 'I've got six now. You don't ask why I am here? How I got here? I came up with Grekky. She is murdering the solicitors. She promised that. One day she will be put away. That is what I have come about.'

I was still considering the phenomenon of the maid with six fur coats when she said that.

I took her remark in the way we understand it; that she thought Mrs Browne would be put into a lunatic asylum.

'Tell me what you mean,' I said and sat down.

'I do not want to go in the slammer,' she said. 'If she goes, I want to be out.'

'You think she might go to prison?'

'Well, what do you think they do to her if they find out all these things she has been going on with?'

'I don't know, because I don't know what she's done.'

She seemed surprised and hesitated a few seconds before going on.

'Oh, I see, but I thought you come to find out all about this.'

'This what?'

'What has been going on!'

'Listen, Anna. Wouldn't it be better if you told me what has been going on and then I might be able to tell you what might happen to her?'

'But if I do that when you don't know it put me in the manoor!'

It seemed she was learning too much of the language from Harry.

'Well, you must make up your mind, Anna. But if you tell me and you don't want anybody else to know, I'll keep it to myself.'

'Yourself, yes.' She looked at the ceiling as if for help, then reached a decision. 'It is about the girl. I do not know what happened to her, but I don't know what happens to the others, either. They always go when I am in bed or away.'

My mind was edging on to the Grand Guignol again, and I tried to stop the garish thoughts. If Arethusa had had lovers they might well have departed quietly and unseen. They did not have to have been murdered, boxed up and buried.

'Do you mean Mrs Browne's niece?'

'Yes. You see, they have such rows. Scream and shouting like mad persons. Then of a sudden she is gone and it worries me because she would have said to me if she went.'

30

Then suddenly her mood changed.

'But I am making a fusspot, bloody stupid. Do not fuss with me. You will give me a drink and I will forget it all.'

I wondered what had come into her mind to make her attitude change so abruptly, but I didn't push because I felt at that time it wouldn't get any result. Either she was too frightened to say any more, in view of the fact that I hadn't known what she was really getting at, or she didn't really know what *had* happened, and thought it wouldn't be a good idea to go on guessing out loud.

I gave her vodka and dry biscuits and she cheered up and became as animated as she had been in her ancient maid's outfit.

I said, 'Are you really her maid, or is it some kind of game?'

'Oh no. She pays,' she said airily. 'I only have to be maid when anybody comes. Rest of the time I do not do much but play games with her and tell fortunes with cards and tea-leaves until sometimes I get creepy because she seems to know so much what will happen. Harry is the working man. He is a bit stupid, but nothing bad.'

'I see. You just play the maid when the visitors come.'

'That is right. Otherwise I am a companion and somebody to swear at. She have to get things off her chest pretty much. Blows up, she says.'

'What sort of visitors are they? Her friends?'

'Some of them is a lot of bloody foreigners,' she said, contemptuously. 'Even blacks and Indian sometimes.'

I thought how odd it was that if I said that it would be illegal, but she, being a bloody foreigner, could say what she liked.

'She said they belonged to sex,' she added. 'But they didn't look very sexy to me. Some of them was old.'

'Sects,' I said. 'Religious people, perhaps.'

'Well, I did not think them very religious either when some of them smack my bum and they are all old and whiskery, I don't know what they expect.'

I wanted to ask, 'And did all these people leave again?' but could not think of a way of putting it so that she would answer.

Yet again, as I sat down, I felt an idiot for keeping on with this ridiculous idea of mass murder. There was no evidence to support it but the woman's lurid story about a mad doctor of a century before.

I said, 'I saw her last night, you know.'

'Yes, I know that.'

'She told me a story about an old doctor in the house who murdered people all the time.'

'Ah yes! Blue beard,' she said, and laughed. 'She is very good with such stories like that.'

'She said that bodies fall out of the cupboards sometimes!' I laughed.

She frowned.

32

'I don't like these stories. Harry says it was one or two doctor's models like the students have.'

'Skeletons?'

'Skeletons, *ja*. Harry says that they may not be real, either, but like mummies. You know mummies with all bandages wrapped up?'

'Yes, I know, Anna. But have you ever seen one of these models?'

'Not me, no. I don't look for such things. We do not sleep in the house.'

I was surprised.

'Where do you sleep, then?'

'There is a little cottage past the pad-dock which is for me to be private, she says. Harry goes to his home which is past the village.'

'Were you ever supposed to sleep in the house?'

'Oh no. She like to be alone there.'

CHAPTER THREE

1

I looked at the pretty woman sitting by my fire, still wearing her rich fur cloak.

'Do you mean you've never spent a night at Cob Weary?' I said.

'Never. I am on my own. She is on her own. Harry is on his own, perhaps. But tonight, it is different. She will not go back there. I know where she is going.'

'And where is that?'

'A flat—apartment, you say?—on a shop which is of a friend.'

'Oh lord! Not a pie shop!' I said, half humorously and fearing it might be one of those truths spoken in jest.

'It sell food. Yes?' She wondered what my remark had meant.

If I said Sweeny Todd and Mrs Lovatt's pies it would have meant nothing to her, and in any case it was a waste of time trying.

'Where is this shop?'

'Along the river at Kingston. You know that?'

'I know that, yes.'

'I give you the address. Of course you know I am a poor girl,' she said with a little wistful look. 'I have to work for my moneys.'

'I'll look after you, Anna. Don't worry.'

She got up and slipped off the cloak.

'Where is the bed, then?' she said, looking round.

'Don't rush things, Anna. Business before pleasure.'

'But it is my business,' she said.

'I mean the business of the address and any other information you have.'

'Oh that,' she said, and pouted. 'This shop—' She stopped and looked at me sharply. 'You are not a bloody copper, are you?'

34

'Of course not. I just want to know where the niece has gone to. She may have something from the will. Of course, don't tell madame that or she might murder everybody.'

'She say the girl went to Greece all of the sudden.'

'Did the girl ever talk of Greece before, do you know?'

'Oh yes, and Hell as well.'

'What do you mean?'

'I mean she say she would sooner go to Hell than stay with Madam Browne. They have rows. You know, when I think, she has rows with all persons. It is like a game of sport with her, I think. You haves people come and then very soon shouting and screaming and terrible noises so sometimes I put cotton wool in my luggoles.'

'Ears,' I said.

'Harry teach me luggoles,' she said firmly. 'And people laugh, so it is all right, eh? You want the address. I have it wrote down in my boozum—' She put a hand down the front of her shirt. I watched, surprised there was room for her hand in there. 'Damn bugger!' she said, pulling her hand out and undoing the shirtfront. 'It is slipped down somewhere. Why can't I do this like the other girls?'

'I think you have to wear a bra to do it properly,' I said, as the shirt came open and revealed, amongst other treasures, a scrap of paper stuck in the waistband of her skirt.

35

'There,' she said, holding it out. 'Do you pay me first? Or do you pay altogether afterwards?'

'Anna, just as you like.' She gave me the paper. 'How did you get this?'

'I write it with a pencil.'

'I mean, where did you see this address, or hear it? Have you been to the place?'

'Yes. She took me once. It is a very old place. She meets people there. She took me to be the maid and look expensive for her. She put on the show for to meet these people.'

'What sort of people?'

'Like I say, all bloody foreigners. All colours. Very depressing. I do not like it there. I think it smells bad. I do not have reasons, but I do not like it there.'

'Does she go often?'

'I don't know that. I am not in the house at night, I tell you that. It is not so far from there. Perhaps an hour but not much more with the car.'

'I see. Now—'

The doorbell rang twice. Anna rose sharply and snatched up the fur cloak.

'It is her!' she whispered. 'Where do I hide myself?'

I pointed.

'Through that door and upstairs. Close the door after you.'

She went at once as if she was practised in carrying out instant dismissals with the

36

minimum of confusion.

It was not the dreaded Mrs Browne at the door, but the tall, smart figure of Miss Jansen, partner in the firm of solicitors dealing with the Browne case.

'Mr Keyes,' she said, almost with relief. 'May I come in? I'm practically exhausted.'

She came in and began explaining almost before I had closed the door.

'That woman! Greco-Browne. A virago! Heavens above! I tell you at one time I was frightened of being shut in the same room with her. You've no idea—! May I have a drink? I'm quite shattered.'

I gave her a strong gin and Italian. She flopped into a chair and appeared, for a moment, to be relieved at being somewhere safe.

'She almost struck me at one point,' she said. 'I think she's a mental case. One moment screaming and shouting and the next arguing almost with calm precision. What do they call that? Manic something or other.' She shivered. 'I feel quite weak.'

'Drink up and calm down,' I said. 'It's over.'

She smiled grimly and shook her head.

'Oh no it isn't! It'll never be over with that woman in the case.'

'I mean that interview.'

'Believe me, I won't see her again on my own. We get some odd characters as you well know, but not raving lunatics. And she does go *mad*. She raves. It's scaring to watch. Specially when you feel you might get murdered in a frenzy—' She looked at her glass. 'No, that sounds idiotically melodramatic. But she could have attacked me. Make no mistake. This is going to be a very difficult matter.'

'But what shot her off like that?'

'Everything. The document, she declared, was a fraud from start to finish. She accused us of trying to find fictitious beneficiaries, holding back the estate in order to do it, manufacturing lies and dead people as claimants—I've forgotten half the things she did scream. The trouble was—and still is—we are trying to find out more and she knows it.'

'Can't she have an advance to keep her quiet? We know she'll get a good deal, no matter who else is found with a claim.'

'She won't have it. She wants the lot handed over at once or sooner. You know the husband's affairs were left in a dreadful mess, but there's money lying about all over the place, and there are still debts which have to be settled. We are the appointed. We can't hand over.'

'Do you think she's frightened that someone else will be found?'

'That's in her mind, which as you know, may have to do with the niece, but there could be others. And there might be a will.'

'You were his appointed, as you say, so why isn't there a will?'

'The one he had, he rejected. He told us things had changed and he wished to alter the whole thing from scratch and any existing wishes scrapped. We were to wait until he gave us the approved version, which never came to us, but it might be lying around in one of his several abodes.'

'Have you any idea what this woman intends to do once she gets this estate?'

'There is a rumour she might just disappear and enjoy life under another name. Amongst other uncivil failings she has, is extreme bitterness against almost everybody. She has a very big problem. I wouldn't like it myself.'

I told her about the way the woman dressed up to soothe sudden wishes and then, the wish salved, undressed again.

'I'm not a psychiatrist,' she said. 'But there must be a word for that, something to do with Vestite.'

She was calming down. I decided not to mention anything about the bodies in Cob Weary. I did not think she was quite in the mood for things like that.

I was not feeling very easy about Mrs Greco-Browne, because once Anna had put the idea into my head that she might call, I wondered how Miss Jansen would react if she did turn up. I didn't want any feminine battles in my expensive house, where some fine pieces of porcelain and glass would never survive warfare.

'You didn't come here to get rid of a nightmare,' I said. 'What do you want me to do?'

'First I think it's important to find where the girl is.'

'But it's said she's in Greece. There isn't much point in going out there without some other clue.'

'Of course not. The fact is, I don't believe a word the woman said. I don't think she is in Greece. We'd like you to find out without anything becoming public.'

'Of course. I'll do my best, but what do you know about the woman? There's something more to your anathema than a row in your office this afternoon. What is known? She hasn't a record, has she?'

'No. We have no information like that.'

'Then what's she been doing? She parted from the husband years ago, didn't she?'

'Ten years. No, she seems to have moved about the country buying up ramshackle old houses with the idea of putting them back into shape, only this doesn't seem to have happened. Two that she bought she bulldozed after she failed to get money enough to do the renovations.'

'She bulldozed? Then what?'

'Sold the land for development, cheap. The locations were so lonely—like this place in Kent—that there isn't much hope of developing until travel gets a lot cheaper than

40

it is now.'

My mind was swimming with pictures of bodies hidden in walls and cellars and I couldn't quite get rid of them.

'What do you really think she was up to?'

Miss Jansen shook her head.

'She might have been quite honestly trying to do what she said. On the other hand—'

'On the other hand? Yes?'

'Well, she may have been up to something that could be quite eccentric, that we wouldn't think of, but I've heard no rumour of the sort you obviously hope for.' She smiled.

I told her about Cob Weary and the story of the lost bodies.

'Oh, no!' she said, and laughed. 'Surely nobody can believe a thing like that!'

'Well, things like that have happened,' I said.

'Yes, they have. But in this case what on earth for? The woman wants the money. Her plans have consistently failed for lack of it. Where on earth's the money in a private graveyard?'

'Where, indeed?' I agreed.

2

Miss Jansen went after asking very carefully if I thought it possible to keep a close eye on Mrs Greco-Browne and find out what she was up to while they did their utmost to find out as much as they could.

Naturally, I said I would do what I could, because by then I was both fascinated and frightened by the probable activities of the fearsome woman. I also stressed that if I got the whiff of the slightest evil I would hand over to the police.

'It's a pity we can't do that now,' she said, 'but we have no evidence whatsoever except that cock-eyed story you told me. I really wouldn't dare pass that one round.'

She laughed as she went out into the thickening fog.

Anna came back into the room on cue, as if she had been listening at the keyhole.

'I am very hard up with the money,' she said. 'I would earn some by helping you with this finding out, *ja*?'

'It's possible, but you'd be in danger from Mrs Browne, Anna.'

She looked sideways at me.

'I don't know about that,' she said in an odd tone. 'I am not frightened so much as you think. She does not fight with me, you see. I am the only one she does not fight.'

'Why?'

'Perhaps I don't know so much, but you 'ave to 'ave some friend you know. It is no good everybody being enemies. If you are so you might get into the manoor.'

'Don't tell me she's frightened of you?'

'She don't know what I know,' Anna said

briefly. 'I just say nothing. When she blows up to try and make me say, I just keep my damn mouf shut, and she stops blowing and gets friendly, so I know I am on the wicket if I keep it so she don't know.'

'What do you know, Anna?'

'Perhaps I know nothing at all,' she said. 'But when she don't know that, I stay all right. I am not born yesterday.'

'You'd better be careful.'

'I am careful.'

'Will you come with me to Kingston?'

'You pay me?' she said, smiling and slipping her arm through mine.

'Of course,' I said.

*   *   *

We drove out to Kingston through the fog. It was damp and thoroughly unpleasant. The shop was in an old, narrow street near the river. The shop was on the corner of an alley. It was open and a few people were coming and going from it, carrying paper packets of food away with them. We drove slowly by and came to a stop just round the corner.

'It smelt like fish and chips,' I said.

'It is, yes, also bangers and bits of chicken made of cement.'

'You stay there,' I said. 'I'll get some.'

The shop looked inside as if it had been got up as a film set for 1900, with gas lamps and

43

four marble tables with vinegar, salt and
pepper pots on them and ancient bills of the
local variety theatre announcing Dan Leno
and a few other performers dead long before
my time.

There were half a dozen people at the tables
eating chips out of newspaper. They looked
out of date in the place, but quite ordinary and
not interested in me. By the smell I could tell
the cooking was being done in dripping,
instead of the vegetable sump oil in use today.

There was a big woman behind the counter
in a white coat, and with a black straw hat
balanced on top of her head and secured by
long hatpins. She was shovelling chips around
in the hot fat which filled the cooking tank.

'Wot's it, dearie?' she said, keeping
everything into period.

'Chips,' I said. 'For two, please.'

'Salt 'n vinegar on 'em or do your own?'

'You do it, please, Mum.'

She chuckled and started to shake out chips
with a wire ladle. I wondered how on earth
Mrs Browne kept up the appearance of a lady
of importance while sitting in a flat that must
have been rich with the raucous smell of the
cuisine below.

'Doesn't it smell of frying upstairs?' I said.

She shook her head.

I got back in the car and we started eating
chips. They were very good indeed. I was
puzzled by the bona-fide look of the place, the

careful attention to period, the good cooking by traditional means—all these things went against the idea that it was a cover for something else going on behind the carefully dated scenes.

'Does Mrs Browne come here very often?'

'Often? Not that much. No. I think she must make appointments and then come. It is not regular like every Tuesday or something.'

I remembered then that Anna did not know where Mrs Browne was every night. She might have heard of her being about to go out, as she had once taken Anna, but that did not mean Mrs Browne was going to Kingston.

'You find out not much?' Anna said.

'No. It looks quite genuine. I thought it might be a cover for some drug exchange, or something of that kind, but it's a carefully staged period piece.'

She opened the door.

'You don't find much, but I am good and she know me from before, you see.'

I had just time to start saying 'Be careful' when the door shut. She was out of sight round the corner in a second. I decided to wait in the car for ten minutes and go and look if she wasn't back by then. I remembered that she did know the place, and also she seemed strangely confident that Mrs Browne would not harm her.

I had at that time the idea that she would help me in exchange for payment and then help Mrs Browne for more payment.

As I sat there a man came along wearing a duffle coat. He was big and stared at the pavement as if depressed by some problem. He came level with the car and looked towards it briefly. From the street lamp across the road I could see his face.

It was Harry. I was not surprised because we had assumed the woman had come to Kingston that night, and she might well have brought a helper—or bodyguard—with her.

He went round the corner out of sight. I waited. When the ten minutes was up, I got out of the car. As I did, Anna came round the corner. We got back into the car.

'I met 'Arry,' Anna said. 'He haves to wait till the shop shut and then take all the things out of the flat with a van. And when I ask the woman if she is upstairs, she says No and she want to see missus because of getting some rent which she is very mad about. They are doing a fit!'

'A flit,' I said.

'And she said it was Mrs Fisher, and I don't know what she means but she says it is the woman I work for, so the name is wrong, too, you see. It is all frauds, *ja*?'

'It looks like it. What did you say to the woman?'

'I just ask if she is in up there because I think I am supposed to meet 'er and she says she would like to meet 'er also and get some money.'

'Did Harry go in there?'

'No, no, no. 'Arry has the key and waits till the woman goes home, then he goes in. That is the way.'

'How do you know?'

'It is done before, I know.'

The information was interesting. It indicated that Mrs Browne had some kind of business which needed temporary accommodation, preferably free.

'How long has she been coming here?' I said.

'It is free munce, about.'

'And all she does is meet people?' I said. 'Now when you came to be the maid, what did they talk about?'

'You think I listen at keyyoles?'

'Yes.'

'Oh, you are bad!' She laughed and smacked my knee. 'But they don't talk loud. They sort of rumble together. It is difficult to hear much. I hear about boats, but what about them I don't say.'

'You mean you don't know?'

'That is what I say.'

'You didn't hear anything else?'

'I say they mumble. They do not trust me to listen. That is why I don't hear.'

'What time does the shop shut? I didn't see a notice in there.'

'It shut by eleven. That is what happens

47

before. She closes and goes to her home.'

I thought the woman might wait longer in the hope of getting her rent. Now that she had seen 'the maid' turn up she could think the mistress would not be far behind.

There was time to take Anna back to my place and return to Kingston before closing time at the shop. When I suggested this, Anna refused.

'Oh no, I come in this because it is my business. If I am to get a chopper through my head I will want to know what for. So I want to know what happens first.'

'I want to wait till Harry starts the moving job. But what I can't understand is why she takes unfurnished flats and then puts her own stuff in when she means to get out quickly and at night.'

'Oh no, it is furnished with chairs and tables and beds and all that,' she said. 'This is what's hers—The boxes.'

'What sort of boxes?'

'Oh, long boxes. Harry says they're pretty heavy. I think they are filled with all her papers.'

Long, heavy boxes. A strange excitement and nausea flowed in my inside. Long boxes.

More bodies?

My imagination was becoming bizarre.

CHAPTER FOUR

1

I left Anna in the car and walked round the corner into the foggy street where the road lamps glowed as if suspended in murky water. There was still a glow in the top of the fish shop windows, but the blind on the glass door was pulled down showing the Closed sign. I thought perhaps the dull light was some kind of hopeful anti-burglar device.

As I stood on the opposite corner of the alley I heard a vehicle grumbling somewhere down the alley itself. The back of a big truck loomed through the fog as it backed up the lane towards where I stood.

The stop lights shone with sudden brilliance through the mist in the alley. The truck stopped and the rumble of its diesel engine died away. In that odd silence that fog brings, I heard a muffled sound of a door slam and then footfalls on the cobbles.

I saw two men walk round the back of the truck and undo what sounded like chain fastenings of the backdrop. They let down a ramp the end of which rested on the cobbles and faced my way.

It was unmistakably a cattle truck; the

wagon used to carry the stock to market, and there was some sort of farming going on at Cob Weary, over which Harry presided.

One of the men used a key to open a door in the wall a yard or two from the shop window. They went in.

Harry and a friend. What friend? Was there another man in the Browne business? Or had Harry picked him up to carry furniture for a few pounds the job?

To my mind Harry was not the sort who would tangle with real villains, nor would crooks have much time for his slow but violent refusal to do as he was told.

I rather thought that Harry was either very loyal, or enamoured of the strong Mrs Browne and for that reason, he did not believe she was bad.

But again, a man used to carting off cattle to market and so to the slaughterhouse might not be much concerned about carcasses of any animal, whatever the number of legs involved.

I ruminated in this acid and melancholy line while I waited for the removal men to appear again.

They appeared carrying a long box between them. It was difficult to be sure from where I stooped, and with gently moving mist in between me and the action, just what size the boxes were. I thought it would be big enough to hold a dead person. People vary in size in any case, and once dead can be adapted to fit any sort of box—

By which time I was beginning to make myself feel sick in the pit of my stomach, and thought the boxes more likely held papers, details of blackmail victims and other domestic correspondence.

I did realize that fairness did not enter into the thoughts I had then of Arethusa Greco-Browne. My ideas of her villainy were painted from other people's opinions, her own blood and thunder story of the house and a suspicion that she had made an old gentleman push his wife off a cliff.

Of evidence against her or in support of anything against her, I had not a trace. Suppose there was nothing sinister in the whole thing? Her attitude would make her a dead target for unpleasant gossip. She probably tried to stimulate it. Hers was that sort of arrogance.

The two men brought out four boxes, or chests, not at all the same shape but each capable of carrying a body in it. At any rate, I thought so.

Neither of the men seemed to look my way or give any sign that they thought what they were doing might be criminal.

After the fourth box one of the men locked the door again, and they closed up the back of the truck. Then one counted out some banknotes into the hand of the other. That done, the man with the money walked away towards me. I walked back towards the car. As I went I heard the diesel start up again.

I got into the car, slammed the door, started up and moved forward.

'What did you see? Are they chasing you off or something?'

'No. I want to follow the truck if I can.'

I turned left. Ahead a truck came out of a side turn and lumbered on away from us. At one point we closed up enough to read a normal number plate, but this one was a sheet of mud with bits of ghostly figures trying to peer through.

Once out of the town Harry began to drive at more than a smart pace. The high wagon swayed and lurched alarmingly, and the thicker the fog, the faster he seemed to go.

I did not mind following in those conditions, because too many mugs will follow close up behind a fast moving vehicle in fog believing the driver ahead can, by some miraculous means, see where he is going.

In my case I just kept him in view with room enough for any sudden emergency.

'He drives lunaticky,' Anna said. 'I tell him that, but *he* just laughs. She likes to have risks because she is a nut case.'

'Do you think she would murder anybody?' I said, as if it didn't matter much either way.

'Do you mean to be serious or is it a guess game?'

'I mean do you think she could if she wanted

to?'

'Yes. Why not?'

'Why not?' I said, nonplussed, as my main brainwork was concentrating on the Jehu ahead and his death-defying antics.

'If she has a good reason she will. Do you know what?' She pointed at the windscreen. 'He is going back to the Cob. This is the road back, I remember when I can see bits at the side—that gate there—' she tried to point at it as it flashed past us then turned back to me again. 'Yes it is the road back.'

It seemed to me that the end of the journey came abruptly. The fog had been running in patches throughout the journey, sometimes thick, sometimes merely a mist.

We were running into a thicker patch when the stop lights flashed on the truck and a yellow signal flicked through a mud layer and within a second of that, the truck swung off to the right and thundered through a greyish looking gateway. As I slowed down we heard the noise of the engine echoing somewhere and then cut off.

'He's driven into the big barn. We 'ave come!' she said.

In moments of considerable confusion one occasionally notices the smallest distraction. I wondered why she varied the sounding of her aspirates.

I ran on a distance until the fog covered us from sight of the barn and then would have

53

stopped, but she tapped my arm.

'You can take me 'ome it is 'ere almost— Look, look! *Da*! Dere! There!'

I swung across the road and into a lane which turned out to end almost at the front door of a cottage.

'You come in,' she said, getting out. 'I will give you a drink and show you one or two things.'

She got out. So did I. The fog was thick when I looked around, but when I glanced towards the gate I saw the side lights of a car outside the entrance of the lane, or drive, as it turned out to be.

There had been no car in the road when we had turned in. Certainly not one as near to the turning as that. I heard no engine.

'There's a car out there,' I said as she opened the cottage door.

'Oh bugger 'im,' she said. 'He is crawling the curb to think I am alone which I am not, you notice.'

I followed her into the cottage, which consisted of one room running into another and a staircase in the second room running up to the bedrooms.

Anna pulled out a drawer in a dresser and from it took a packet of photographs. She sorted through the pictures and then gave me one of a nude girl wearing a long string of wooden beads standing on a beach with a lot of such ladies sitting and lying round on the sand.

'That is her niece, Lauren Hazel at St Tropez. And that beyond is Our Woman with a hat on her face.'

'Mrs Browne?' I said, looking at the stretched out naked woman behind the girl. I suppose there was nothing surprising about the flamboyant Arethusa spreading herself out on the beach, but what interested me was that the two women were apparently there together. 'When was this taken?' I said.

'I take that in June. Mrs Browne says to me "I will go to St Tropez," and so I say, "Then I go to St Tropez when you pay", and we go. When we get there, so is her niece, already.'

'Was that a surprise?'

'It was to me, but I think she knew first. You keep the picture then you know what she looks like.'

I was putting it in my pocket wallet when the door opened behind me.

'Oh, you're busy, Anna,' said Arethusa, drawling. 'Then I won't interrupt. Good night Anna, good night Mr Keyes.' She turned to go out. 'Oh—while I remember; will you call in the morning, Mr Keyes? There has been a development over the document on which I need some particular advice.'

She went. The door closed. I don't think we spoke until we heard the car start up in the road.

'She comes to see who it is,' Anna said. 'But I think she knew who it is. Perhaps she is

55

beginning to get shook up.'

'Why do you think that?'

'I know her. I know her little movements. She is no secret from me. I can tell when she jumps.'

She got some drinks. I sat on the table looking through the other pictures. Some of them showed up her sense of humour and some were frankly rude, but of the twenty, there were four at the end taken at Cob Weary showing the tithe barn, horses in a field and Harry walking away from them, and on the last, Harry digging in a walked garden.

'How did you come to meet Mrs Browne?' I said.

'That was last year,' said Anna, sitting down with her drink. 'I am this call girl and there is this agent man who is above the board but he knows what goes on sometimes and looks the other way, but he has this call from down Kent, he says, and there are not many girls like to go down Kent, but I am so fed up I go down anywhere.'

'What were you fed up about?'

'Fed up with old men. It is the old men who have the money and I don't want to marry some old bloke for his money because when I get married I am going to be a proper wife an not a peculiar somebody, but you know what I mean.'

I didn't, but preferred not to press.

'What did you find when you got down

56

here?'

She laughed.

'You never believe!'

'Well, what did you find?'

'Arry!' She laughed more. 'Arry the dung-flinger! Me the posh in my evening gown and fur coat and there is Arry!'

Her laughter was infectious. She really enjoyed the joke, as if it made her happy.

'Do you mean he arranged with the agency?'

'No, Mrs Browne. She arranged for a party, but no party comes and I am there all beautiful looking at Arry in gumboots and funny hat from milking cows!' She went off again.

When she recovered, I made my point.

'But you stayed,' I said, and saw her watch me sharply. 'Why on earth did you?'

At that moment, when I really wanted to know, somebody started banging on the door with a brick, it sounded like.

2

I looked at Anna. She looked at the door.

'Arry!' she shouted, and then gave instructions in Harry-like language for him to depart with speed and direction.

Harry opened the door and stuck his head in. Anna, with the speed of a professional cricketer, snatched off one of her shoes and shied it at Harry's head. It hit the wall as the door shut.

57

'I stand no nonsense,' said Anna, sitting back with satisfaction.

'Anna! I gotter talk!' Harry burbled through the wood.

'You do not have to talk. I am deaf tonight!' Anna shouted, and added further instructions on one way he could go.

I heard him start walking away and then stop.

'He hasn't gone,' I said, quietly.

'No. He sits outside like some stupid great dog to protect me. He is a big soft Fanny.'

'You like him?'

'Oh yes. He appeals to my rude side. I feel young and naughty like a girl doing what I wasn't supposed. And when I see that he is all there is that night I laugh, but I like his smell. He smell of man, you know? He don't smell of all scents and shaves and stinky things, so it was like back at home, so I like it.'

'But that isn't why you stayed?' I said, cautiously.

'Oh, no!' She laughed again. 'No I stay because she offers me money, of course, and it is for doing nothing much at all.'

'She pays you well?' I was surprised.

'More than I could make with my profession . . .'

'For doing nothing?'

'I pretend to be a maid, you know, and we play chess and so forth, and I stop her doing herself in.'

58

That startling end to the list of her duties shook me.

'Do you mean she might commit suicide?'

'Oh yes.' She sounded as if that was quite a normal wish for any grown person to have from time to time. 'Now and again she says "Hold my hand from my frote". That is when she holds a knife for cutting the cheese or something. She get very entangled with herself sometimes. She gets very down in the dump. In the manoor, you know. Then she gets very funny, but not to laugh at.'

'Do you think she's a little mad?'

'No, no. She is very sane, but sometimes she gets working it all out where it will end and it don't look as it will be the right end and she gets very black then. So I take the good hold of her and say "You sit still, you silly bitch", to comfort her till she feels better.'

She had then taken the odd shoe off and had her feet tucked up under her. She frowned.

'I worry for her in case she is bad for certain.'

'You sometimes think she is?'

'No, I think it all the time, I think. I don't know what she is playing at and it could be very bad because that is why she suddenly thinks to cut her frote and that. I think she wants to do it suddenly when she think somebody else might want to do it for her first.'

Once again the brick-like fist of Harry smote the panels.

'She's comin'!' He hissed through the door crack like an escape of boiler steam.

I heard him move quickly away and then become still as if he waited out there to watch what went on.

Mrs Browne called before she got to the door, as if she fancied Anna might as well be upstairs as down.

'I'm in here!' Anna shouted, without moving from her chair.

The door opened. This time the big woman came in.

'I am not feeling well, Anna. Not well at all,' she said, ignoring me entirely. 'I hear people talking about me.'

'I tell you there is no person talking,' Anna said firmly. 'You imagine such things with yourself.'

'Comfort me, Anna. Comfort me.'

She sounded as if she would start to cry. She went to Anna's chair, holding out her hands.

The change was so violent from the woman I had met I was bewildered. I even wondered for a moment whether it was the same woman; as if there might be a twin I hadn't seen till then.

'Go up to bed,' Anna said. She got up and kissed the woman, then turned her by her outstretched hands towards the stairs. 'I will come to you in a moment.'

'I am sad, Anna.'

'Yes, yes. You are sad. You go and I will see that you sleep.'

'No, no. You come to me. I'll go back now to my house. You come to me.'

'I will come.'

The woman turned. She looked at me for an instant, then deliberately turned away to the door and went out. We heard her move away. Anna went and opened the door.

''Arry, go back with Mrs Browne.' She shut the door and turned to look at me. 'She has been taking things. I known when it is like this. She is cokey.'

'Does it happen often?'

'No. But sometimes when she gets very sad like I told you.'

'When she might kill herself?'

'Yes, yes. Like that.' She put her shoes on then and straightened. 'You take me up there, then you stay as well.'

'She was all right a quarter of an hour before,' I said.

'Yes. I don't know how it comes but it does. I am sure she takes things, but I never see it, so I cannot say for sure.'

'These must be difficult times for you.'

'No. When it comes like this she does what I tell her like a child. Sometimes I think it is to get sympathy she threatens to cut her frote and drown herself. I never believe what she says, but I could not risk to be wrong in case she did it, you see?' She got her coat round her shoulders. 'We go.'

We went. I drove back through the fog to the front of the house and we went in. The front door was wide open when we got there.

'I'll kill you, Harry!'

'I done what you said, now I'm going ter get sleep. I need sleep. I look like I'll get three hours afore the milking so you get your bed and I'll get mine.'

'You refused me!'

'Shut it down!' Harry bawled.

There was silence as we went into the big room.

'I'll kill you!' Mrs Browne cried, with intense passion in her voice.

Harry's answer was to slam a door behind him.

Anna went to the dazed woman.

'I take you up. Come along.'

At first the woman did not seem to see Anna, but then she turned as directed.

'I will kill Harry, when he has finished the cows tomorrow,' Mrs Browne said and walked away with Anna.

I did not think the big woman had seen me at all. She seemed at that time to be out of touch with what was really going on. I thought her behaviour was due to drugs, but couldn't guess what sort. Her appearance at that time was more like a person who had lost the hinges which should have joined her to the real world.

But it is very difficult to be sure with people whose belief in life is that nobody else counts at all except when needed for assistance.

Yet every time I came into this barn of a house I began to have doubts about the reality of anything. Or perhaps I mean honesty, rather than reality.

That night, for instance, the woman had appeared to us as normal, but fifteen minutes later, she had seemed either drugged to the eyebrows or off her rocker.

I know an actress who can do that sort of thing so convincingly that she can—and does—frighten a whole party into goosepimples by her apparent loss of grip on her moral sanity.

Arethusa also had many parts to her performance, starting with the horsey whip wielder I had first seen, to going as the grande dame of the same evening, then the virago I had heard of the following afternoon, then the calm businesslike woman of that night, and now, suddenly, a half crazed dope-taker seemingly dependent on Anna's strength for support.

Did she put on these theatrical attitudes as she felt like it? If so it might be a method of keeping Anna by frightening her into thinking the woman might really kill herself if Anna went.

But why try it on me? Why that lost, drivelling performance of a helpless woman who a moment before, when she'd thought herself unobserved, had vented direct wrath on Harry the Unwilling?

There had been nothing for her to gain by showing me her many melodramatic facets. In fact, they might only make me more suspicious than I already was.

But then again, doubt entered my mind. She had blazed at Harry, then when he had gone, seemed stunned until Anna had taken her arm, but even then, she had said, in almost a distant tone, that she would kill Harry after he had milked the cows the next morning.

If that had been acting, it was very good stuff indeed. As I thought of it I was reminded of the wandering woman in a nightdress wishing by candlelight to out the damned spot.

But Lady Macbeth had had her laird to do her strong arm stuff. Arethusa Greco-Browne seemed to have the male strength rolled up in her; a villain all complete in one woman.

Again I felt ashamed of my bias against the woman which still had no evidence to back it, or even enough to excuse it.

As I stood there the door crashed open and Harry reappeared.

'Where she gone?' he said, stopping and looking round.

'She isn't well. Anna's taken her to bed.'

'She's not well! What about me? Humpin' her bloody boxes about half the night and drivin' in the bloody fog for miles till I get cross-eyed and I gets back here and she wants me for this that and the other and I got bloody cows at six. I'm chuckin' this lot in, I am. I'd sooner die of old age than get worn down to me bloody knees by thirty. What's she want done with them boxes? It's market tomorrow. I got to use that wagon. She gives me the gobbles, she does.'

'Can't you move the boxes?' I said, with some cunning.

'Takes two, them boxes. I have to have help.'

'Well, who helped you?'

'Sid, but he lives up Kingston. I ain't got nobody about 'ere like that. Less you want to give me a hand.'

'I'm not a weight lifter.'

'Sid's no weight lifter, neither, but he can put his pound to the lift when he wants to and has the lolly for it. I don't know why she keeps him on, stuck up there doing nothing all day long. I don't make out what he's there for, when there's me down here sloggin' away like a navvy morn, noon and night. I'd pee off if 'tweren't for the cows come six tomorrer. They has to have somebody else they suffers, and there's nobody 'ere that's like to look to their sufferin's, I tell you, mister.'

Then suddenly he seemed to realize he was talking to me and not to some friend of his. He stared at me.

'How come she let you in this time o' night?' he said, and looked towards the door by which the women had gone out of the room. 'She muss be ill.'

This thought made him frown at the floor, and then he turned and thumped out, slamming the door behind him, as was his custom.

CHAPTER FIVE

1

After the fading thunder of Harry's departure had gone, the place fell suffocatingly quiet. I wondered what had happened to the two women. I felt I should have heard some sound of movement from upstairs, but there was none.

I had a profound uneasiness about that house at any time, but in the middle of the night, alone by a candlelight which hardly reached the corners of the big room, *and* in an unnerving silence, the place felt actively sinister.

To comfort myself I thought again about my actress friend who could switch from anarchy to sanity with the flick of a false eyelash. I tried to ponder the difference between anarchy and banality and came up with 'when churchyards yawn and graves give up their dead', and started imagining corpses toppling out of secret openings beginning to yawn in the cobwebbed walls.

This bloody reverie was interrupted by a distant cry for help. I was relieved to hear it. There was no doubt it was Anna, for the caller was undecided about which language to shout it in, but the tone was unmistakable.

I ran across to the door through which the women had gone and found myself in a sort of passage with a hefty flight of bent oak stairs leading up. There was a candle in a heavy stick standing on the table at the foot of the stairs and I took it with me, as upstairs seemed to be in pitch darkness.

This sudden activity smothered the gruesome imagery which had been invading my mind a few seconds before. I moved fairly fast up the stairs to keep the bad dreams well behind me.

But at the top of the stairs there was silence. I stood and peered around the landing which seemed to be enclosed by brown bulging walls supported by black timber framing. Further away from the stairhead I could just see a couple of heavy doors obviously leading to bedrooms.

The passage also ran the other way past the stairhead, and I just had to guess where the scream had come from. To the right, I reckoned, the rooms lay above the big room downstairs and a sound from there was most likely to be heard below. I therefore went that way, but stopped when I got to the first door.

The silence was deafening. I thought I should be hearing something but the dead quiet was stuffing my ears with wool. I tried the door handle, and stood for a second when I found the door unlocked. Then I pushed it open. I had to put the candle ahead of me before I could see much in the gloom, but I did see it was a bedroom and nobody was in it. An overturned vacuum cleaner suggested this was the guest room where Harry had gone on strike.

The important point was that Anna was not there and I went to the next door. As I opened that one, I heard a thump like a door slamming from somewhere in the darkness of the room. I held the candle up and looked round.

There were two cupboard doors beyond the bed, which was rumpled about as if someone had been in it and got up in a great hurry.

A cadaver, perhaps, not wanting to be seen in his ugly state. My grisly period was coming back as I went across to the cupboard side of the bed. I hesitated at the first door, and listened, but the silence was everywhere.

The obvious thing for me to do was to thump on the doors and shout 'Anna!' That might be heard even if she were not in this room or part of it. But the idea of making a row frightened me, as if to draw attention to myself would make me a target.

Carefully I opened a cupboard door a little

68

then pulled it wide very quickly. Inside was a pile of woman's clothes tumbled on the floor almost as if a woman was inside them. I opened the second cupboard and the contents of that surprised me.

There were some saws, some standing against the back wall, some lying on the floor with chisels and other carpenter's tools. The presence of such things in a bedroom merely sharpened my bloody imagination.

As I went back to the door I thought, more reasonably, but the tools might have been needed to mend the bed. Perhaps the dressing-table had broken a leg or something. There could be a dozen useful reasons for the tools being there without thinking of dismembering bodies.

There were no more calls for help. I began to think of Anna having been murdered and dripping blood all over the floor, wherever she was.

That damned house—and it felt damned—got one by the nerves and poured horror into the open ends. One could not look in any direction without being surrounded by evil, either of the past or the present.

There were no more doors ahead. I went back past the stairhead and found two doors opposite each other across the corridor.

There was still nothing to hear, until, as I paused at the left-hand door I heard a faint, rhythmic squeaking from behind it.

I felt an odd kind of relief at hearing something. It meant that everything in the place wasn't dead.

I got the handle, turned it right back and with a slight motion made sure the door was then free. I waited a second then swung the door open sharply.

There was a brief, incredible glimpse of someone hanging by a rope from the ceiling, and then the sudden backdraught from the opening door blew my candle out.

I felt for the door-post and then moved behind it. I don't smoke but I carry a lighter sometimes for social purposes. I did not even know if I had it that night.

As I felt one-handedly in my pockets there was no sound of movement but the creaking of the twisting and untwisting rope.

The faint shape of a window at the end of the passage just showed in the dark, but that was all the light in the world there was just then.

The brief flash of that dreadful sight was stuck on my retina as bright as a picture on a wall, but one thing about that scene was peculiar.

It seemed to me, while I fumbled for a lighter, that a hanging man's head turns very sharply down. This man's head was upright as if the suspending rope went down through his skull.

Nausea hit me again and brought a clammy

sweat with it. I did not know what sort of icy-nerved heroes hunted around for corpses in places like this, but they weren't like me.

I found my lighter and flicked the switch. As soon as the little light flared I put it to the candle wick. The lights though very small were blinding in the darkness.

My hand shook on the candlestick as I thought what I had lit the light for. Because I didn't want to see it again I argued with myself as to whether it could have been real, or some curious kind of hanging fruit basket or sling which in the quivering light of the candle had seemed to take the brief shape of a hanging man.

The swift defences of the mind in flashing together walls of excuse are wonderful to consider. I often marvelled at it and wished them strong enough to imagine me right out of the situation, but it never has. With that realization in mind I steadied my hand and turned to peer into the room.

When I did my senses almost froze. That man hanging from the beamed ceiling by the top of his shrunken head was but one of four or five.

The scene of such terrifying figures, slowly turning to and fro in the flickering light of a candle was the stuff of nightmare.

When a scream from the corridor behind me called for help I was momentarily glad that such an interruption could swing me round to a direct thought which almost hived off the mental scene of the death room.

I ran. I was glad to run away, but also I wanted to get Anna out of the danger she was obviously in. Too long had passed already.

I had run two or three paces towards the stairs when I realized that there was but one room I hadn't looked in—that was directly opposite the dreadful room I had run from.

It was strange, because the sound had seemed to come from that other direction which I had started on, but I ran back to the one remaining unopened door. By that time I felt whoever was menacing Anna would guess somebody was about trying to find her. There was no secret about me being in the house that night.

I opened the door firmly. There was candlelight in the room.

Only one person was in that room and that was Mrs Browne, fast asleep on the bed and covered with a fur coat. There were no cupboards. I went to the bed and shook her shoulder but she was flaccid and too deeply asleep to wake up.

It seemed that Anna must be somewhere downstairs after all, although I would have sworn the screams had come from upstairs.

From the time I'd heard the first one to when I stood by the sleeping woman was about two minutes. An awful lot can happen in that time.

I went and closed the door behind me and headed for the stairs. Half way down I heard Anna scream again. I ran down, shielding the candle flame with one hand and went once more into the big room.

As I got inside the door Anna came flying out of the darkness into the pale of my candle, which was then the only light in that room.

She cried out something in a panic-stricken voice as she clutched out to me, but as she said it in German I didn't understand.

In the shadow behind her I saw someone going quickly away towards the main exit from the room. I could not see who it was, but I could see it wasn't Harry. The figure was too thin.

She clung to me.

'He's got away!' I said. 'Let go!'

She wouldn't. I didn't want to chase the man, since she didn't seem hurt, but I did want to know who he was.

There was not supposed to be an odd man about that house that night.

I tried to stop Anna crying on my coat front.

'What happened?' I asked, two or three times.

At last she choked on her tears and said something I had heard before.

'He tried to cut my frote.'

'He had a knife?'

'Not first,' she said breathlessly and let me go at last. 'I comed out from missus and he is

73

waiting and try to get me, but I run like beggary and scream. But he don't notice and runned after me and went I got down the kitchen stairs I falled down and then I get up he have me round the frote and pick zis knife off the table and put it across my frote to stop the scream or he will do me in!'

'How did you get away?'

'I could not at the first because he haves this knife right on my frote, but in my business— when I was—I haves some funny customers sometimes and I have a special kick which make them let go so when he took it away a little bit to ask some questions I give him this kick and he let go all right, and I run then and you come.'

'Did you see who it was?'

'No, because always he is behind.'

'I see. What did he ask you?'

'He ask who was you—who you was,' she said. 'He kept on but when I say, he says I am a liar—'

She caught hold of me again and began to sob quietly on my coat.

'Oh dear,' I thought.

2

As I stood there letting her spend her emotional build-ups on my coat, I wondered what on earth to do about that fearful room upstairs. The more I returned to that awful scene in my mind the more details I remembered.

The bodies had dripped into bowls on the floor set under their hanging feet. The dripping had stopped or I would have heard it, and the bowls were part full of dark liquid.

As I stood there holding a warm human body the scene of that room appeared more and more grotesque. I began not to believe it; I didn't want to. My mind began searching round for explanations that might fit that private charnel house.

Then a thought made me wonder if what I had seen was really what it looked like. Bluebeard's Room had been kept locked for obvious reasons. Then why was this one unlocked, as if it didn't matter who looked in?

I might have been half expected to look in, especially as I had been invited to spend the night. I could have wandered about looking for a bathroom and opened that door by mistake—

I began to realize that the unlocked door might indicate that nobody cared who saw inside, and that if he did he would never get out to tell anyone, but would end up with a hook through his skull, slowly turning as he dripped his blood into a bowl underneath his feet.

Then supposing that they had not been recent corpses but some of these found in the walls, dead two hundred years, or whatever the

75

story was?

All the same one has to report such finds. One cannot enter into one's diary things like; 'Yesterday afternoon three old corpses fell through the study ceiling on to my desk and upset the ink: I got the gardener to bury them by the compost heap.'—and leave it at that.

Impossible. Ridiculous. But from the attitude of the lady of the house this is mostly what she did think of the long dead.

Of course, I could see the argument about people unwinding mummies and Jeremy Bentham and medical student's bones. These were widely known matters. I also recalled some cemetery by Oxford where all the bodies had been shovelled up and put in another place because their last resting places were needed for a by-pass. All these things were all right because there were legal papers making everything all right.

Mrs Browne had no legal papers. As bodies fell out of the wainscoting so she had them disposed of, she said.

Then what were these dreadful things doing hanging there, draining? Draining what?

Anna pushed me back.

'I am better,' she said, with a slight sniff.

With the macabre picture of that room in my mind Anna's attacker had become slightly unimportant.

'Has anybody got into the house before at night?' I said.

'I don't know because mostly I am not here, you remember.'

'Has Mrs Browne ever said anything about people getting in?'

'She would not tell. She only talks about herself and not anybody else.'

'There's a room opposite her bedroom.'

'Oh yes. That's where she dries her things.'

'What things, Anna?'

'I don't know. Her personal things I suppose. I don't know. It is always locked.'

'Always?'

'Always, always,' she said rather impatiently.

'This evening, Anna, when you had put her on the bed, what did you do?'

'I cover her up with one of my old coats and come out and shut the door, then the man come up behind me and I scream. Like that.'

'I see. So you've never seen in the locked room?'

'No, I do not want to see in her private places. If she don't want to see me looking, then I don't want to look.'

'What sort of voice had he got?'

'It was mostly whisper, like hissing. He didn't want you to hear him of course. But he had a cuff-link with a dragon on it. That I can see when he is shoving his hand over my mouf before he got this knife.'

'He didn't want me to hear him?'

'Of course.'

'How did he know I was here?'

My theory was that he had been in the death room with the door shut when he had heard people come into the house. Perhaps he had heard Harry's stentorian tones and knew that somebody must have been downstairs for him to use them at.

Then I thought he might have heard someone come in, and peered down through slits between the ancient floorboards, which would have let him look directly into the big room and see who had come in there.

In which case he must have known the house very well.

'You come with me and I get coffee,' she said, grabbing my hand.

We went together out to the kitchen. It was a large kitchen with a cooker that was going at some pace, judging by the heat dial on the front of the oven.

She made some instant coffee. In view of the nervous strain I was suffering, I suppose, it tasted quite acceptable.

'You are very thoughtful,' she said, watching me.

'I have a lot to think about,' I said.

That was true. I did not know what to do about that awful room.

The story of corpses in this house was widespread. It was as good a joke as any in the village, and probably with the police, too. I supposed then—and do now—that if you want to start on a career of mass murder by finding

78

victims nobody knows, then the best thing to make sure everybody minds their own business is to spread the news of your intention around a small community. If you don't get put away for treatment, you will be treated—and left alone—as a gentle lunatic or hoaxer, whatever the difference is.

If I went to the police with the story of what I had seen they might begin to suspect pottiness in me, or more likely, had heard it before from others.

Further, the private detective may be highly respected in fiction, but in fact the police are not receptive to being told wholesale slaughter has taken place on their doorstep while they have been escorting political demonstrations.

Especially when the information is part of a hoary old tale that had been a queasy joke around the district for many years.

It might be more efficient for me to use my firm to contact the Browne solicitors and for them to ask the police to investigate.

But when they heard my account of what I had seen they might well consider the matter at some length before they acted. In short, they wouldn't believe it because they had heard it all before.

As I sat on the table drinking hot coffee I found I was beginning to doubt exactly what I had seen and was searching in my mind for something innocuous to explain it.

My mind turned from the gory spectacle and

fixed on the reason why the intruder had gone to see it. If that room had always been kept locked then he had a duplicate key or he could pick locks.

And having seen the secret of the room, he had then come straight out and captured Anna coming out of the bedroom. Having done that his main interest, so Anna said, was who I was.

It seemed to indicate he knew I was a stranger, so he knew who might normally be expected to be calling at the house.

Further it was pretty plain that he knew his way about in the building, and since the place was higgledy-piggledy with bits added on and others knocked off over centuries, I thought it would take a little knowing.

From his behaviour I could think of only one reason for it, and that was blackmail.

In that case he would expect very good payments, because keeping corpses was an expensive secret by any standards, and therefore I had to assume he knew about the money which Mrs Browne expected to control before long.

Then an alternative suggested itself.

'Does Mrs Browne have any business friends? People who do business when they come here?'

'She has men who talk. I suppose it is business. I never stay to listen, so I don't know much.'

'What is her business? Farming?'

'It is farming, yes. Herself with Harry do most but sometimes they haves men from the village and around. I do not know if it makes the money, but there's always money about.'

'Lying about?'

'Sometimes. To pay the people in the village, the bread and butcher and that. She pays when they come like a poor person.'

'But she didn't pay the rent at the fish shop,' I said.

'That is because it is not next door and she could get away with it. She is very mean if she can get away with it.'

'When did you first hear about old dead bodies being hidden in the house? Can you remember?'

She laughed then.

'I remember it is all to make people shiver. There was some old mad doctor once, but it was long before my great grandfather, perhaps, and somebody make up these stories about him and bodies and Dracula and everything. It is all rubbish. She frightens people with it to make her laugh.'

Anna was quite firm.

'So you've never seen anything like it here?'

'Would I stay? Not much, I tell you! No bloody fear. I seen a skeleton like the students have in a cupboard because Harry found it, but it is all held together with a lot of strings or wires or something and people do not hold together by things like that.'

'But Harry doesn't like it?'

'Harry is very suspicious. If he sees a magpie he spit for good luck because if he don't spit it's bad luck, he says, but if it two magpies, that's a good luck and you don't spit. Now how do you make any sense of that?'

'And he thinks skeletons are bad luck?' I said.

'He don't like them. Nor do I, but it don't make bad luck. All the bad luck is what the skeleton had.'

I let her talk for a little while so as not to push one line too far in case she clammed up. When she got another cup of coffee for herself I opened a new avenue.

'Does Mrs Browne take anything for her nerves?'

'Oh, she take some drug or other. It don't seem to do her temper much good.'

'She gets them from her doctor?'

'She never goes to the doctor. She don't like doctors.'

It then began to appear that, on top of all the other suspicions I had of her, Mrs Browne was also a dealer in drugs. Hence the dealing with foreigners in far-away flats.

I remembered a snippet of conversation I had heard at a police station, when the constable said, 'She can't be all bad.'

The sergeant said, 'She can.'

CHAPTER SIX

1

The gloom of the big, candelit kitchen appropriately distorted the thoughts of my position. There was no phone in this place, therefore the proper course seemed to be to go away and call the police.

At that time, and talking to Anna, I couldn't picture myself confronting a well-trained critical police officer with a story of five corpses suspended by their skulls and draining off into basins on the floor. I felt such a story would not carry too well.

It was then, when imagining myself trying to put it across to a quietly interested policeman, that I began to realize I couldn't believe it myself.

They couldn't be corpses. They had to be dummies of some sort. Artists' fixable models, perhaps, which can be switched into any pose as required.

But why they should all be required just to hang from a hook by their toupées was beyond my powers of invention to answer.

And why were they all wet?

'Does Mrs Browne draw or paint? Anything artistic?'

'Oh a bit now and then, perhaps. She start something, get off her hook and stamps on it or tears it up. She does it to make herself cross, I think.'

'She paints scenery?'

'Oh no, people. People doing things, you know.'

'Action pictures?'

'Oh yes, very much action, but she don't do it often. Not like an artist. My father was an artist, Mama says, but he rubbed himself out of her picture, she says, too.'

I was thinking that if I went to the police I should have to have a normal sort of criminal story to present first. That way they could be persuaded to come, look into things, and then go from horror to horror until they were up to their knees in blood.

Undoubtedly, that was the practical way to do it.

The first thing, then, was to find some evidence which was reasonably credible but which would be enough to draw them in.

The boxes Harry had collected. Perhaps we could find something incriminating there.

Anna was watching me sharply.

'What you going to do?' she said. 'I can see you plotting.' She pointed at me.

'I was thinking I ought to see what's in the boxes Harry brought back,' I said. 'I'll have to get a torch from the car first.'

'You don't leave me 'ere!' she said, firmly. 'I

don't know where that man went.'

'He ran out,' I said, but of course, I wasn't sure of that. He'd just run into the darkness and might be somewhere there still.

We went out to the front door with the help of the candle.

It was not dark outside, but still foggy. A moon was somewhere overhead making the fog light grey all round. I could see quite a few yards all round. As I opened the car door to get my torch, I saw across the car to the rear window, and thought for a moment, I must be mistaken.

We had come in by a wide opening in the high hedge where once a gate had been hung. I could see the upper outline of the hedge still, but no gap where we could have come in.

I got the torch, straightened up, closed the car door and then looked at the hedge again.

It was a misty vision, true, but there was no lighter gap in the dark outline of the hedge. Someone had closed the escape gateway.

My interest quickened. I went to the back of the car and pretended to look at something there. Again I looked at the hedge and being closer, could see that where the gap had been there was now some sort of heavy vehicle closing the way.

There was no sound of an engine. The thing was just stuck there to seal up the gap.

I had never seen another way out of the overgrown surround to the house, and a foggy

85

night was no time to try and find one. The car therefore, had to be left where it was for the time being.

It was not an easy thought, that a quick way out was now closed. As I went back to the house door I tried to comfort my uncertain self by thinking that perhaps the lorry was stuck in the gate by accident. Perhaps it had been turning, got stuck, and broke down in the gap.

Anna had watched me, but she had not been able to see as far as the hedge from the doorway, so I said nothing of the jammed gap.

What I did say was to tell her to light every candle we passed and get some light into the place. By the time we left the big room for the kitchen the place was glowing with the clusters of small, warm, light pools. For some reason, that pretty glow made me feel better. The slight warmth in my soul vanished when I looked out of the back door into the foggy yard.

The place seemed full of shadows, so that it was difficult to make out what anything was. I could not even make out the great tithe barn amongst the looming ghosts around that brick-paved yard.

'I come with you,' she said from behind me.

'Where's the barn?'

'There. *Da.*'

'Isn't that Russian?'

'What? The barn? I don't know.'

We were speaking very quietly, because the

86

night had that sort of feel to it; as if it might be listening.

After seeing the lorry stuck out in the front hedge, I felt that somebody else might be listening, also.

She led me across the yard to where I could see the barn dead ahead, the doors wide open. We went inside before I shone the torch.

It looked as if Harry had thought about unloading the truck, for the back was let down and we could see inside it. The boxes were still there, so it looked as if Harry had changed his mind and left unloading till the morning.

As I went towards the truck, she caught my arm.

'There is some car in the gate,' she whispered.

I turned and peered out. A car was barely visible through the fog, but it was there all right, front almost against the five-bar gate, it seemed, so the rest of it must have slewed across the opening.

'Who are they?' she whispered again.

'I don't know.'

It really wouldn't have been much help if I had known, because the vehicles certainly didn't belong to the police, and so had to be assumed unfriendly.

But unfriendly against whom? That question seemed to offer a chink of hope in the foggy night. They might not be interested in us, but only with Mrs Browne, or with the man who had been in the house that night.

I listened very carefully, but the night was as still as it had been in the house.

The quiet was so intense I began to think there was no one in the car. It had been left there so that no vehicle could get out. What made me think the car was empty was that we should have been heard crossing the yard to the barn and that, as there had been no reaction, there was probably no one there to react.

I told Anna what I thought and after a very cautious consideration, she seemed to agree.

It seemed likely now that if we tried to get out past either of the blocking vehicles, alarm might be raised, and there was no point in taking a risk of being mistaken for somebody else and getting hammered for it.

But we were within touching distance of the mysterious boxes and my curiosity was then intense. What made it so I don't know, because all I really wanted to know was that the boxes were *not* filled with human remains. I needed that information for my immediate peace of mind, a peace that might finally persuade me that the macabre scene in the hanging room had been a parade of waxworks and no more.

I got up into the truck. She stayed by the end of the ramp looking up. I shone the torch round the boxes. They did look like straight-sided coffins. The lids were fixed with hasps and small padlocks. I have a small instrument which can undo certain types of lock, but only about one in every ten locks. It is no good for stealing cars. These padlocks were all different, as if Mrs Browne had bought a job lot cheap along with even cheaper hasps.

Investigation showed it would be quicker to unscrew the hasp fixings than mess about trying to pick the locks. I began to unscrew the plate on the nearest box to the front, so that not much light went out the open back of the truck.

The screws were tight in and my screwdriver—a part of my penknife—small, so work was slow. As I carried on the job, a freezing thought came to me: supposing, instead of finding peace inside, there was another corpse?

Immediately I comforted myself with the thought that such things wouldn't have been left in an open barn.

But there were five bodies swinging about in an open room.

I heard her hiss, 'Are you all right?'

She was worried. I told her I wouldn't be much longer. She gave some sort of sigh and was quiet again. I went on unscrewing with the little screw-driver blade slipping out of the screw cut as often as it was in it. Difficulties make for tension. I felt more and more tense the longer the unscrewing took. I broke off once to try my lock prodder, but that only wasted more time.

When at last I had the screw out I remained squatting there beside the box, too tensed up to open the lid and see what the answer really was.

''Aven't you done it?' she hissed anxiously.

She had come up to the top of the ramp, almost in the truck.

'Just going to,' I said, and straightened up.

I got the fingers of both hands under the edge of the lid and lifted. It didn't want to come. I pulled harder. The wood started to creak, but still it didn't come loose.

With the torch I bent and examined the under edges of the lid, but could see nothing that was holding it. I straightened and tried again.

The lid seemed to lift a bit then go back, as if stuck to rubber inside. I straightened again.

'What's the matter?' She was getting agitated.

'It's stuck somehow,' I said. 'I can't lift it.'

'I get a chisel,' she said. 'There is one in the kitchen.'

I saw her turn round on the ramp to go down it, but then she stopped.

'No, not alone. You come.'

To go with her was all I could do because I couldn't move the lid. We went.

When we got back I went up the ramp and into the truck.

The lid was off and lying on the floor. The box was empty.

I shone the torch in the box. I shone it all round the inside of the truck and saw only other boxes and the usual straw bits lying around the floor, marks of its usual occupation of carrying animals.

She stood at the top of the ramp looking at me.

'What's the matter now? What's inside?'

'Nothing. It's empty. The lid fell off.'

'You are crazy!'

'No. It's true.'

She came into the truck then, to see for herself. Then she crouched down and looked closely.

'There is blood here,' she said, looking up. 'Do you cut yourself?'

'No.' I went down beside her and looked inside the box at the side where the lock had been.

There was blood, as she said, which seemed to have run down the side, staining the wood for two or three inches.

'Somebody was 'olding the lid shut on you,' she said. 'That is what!'

Somebody inside, holding the lid shut while I tried to lift it. The idea seemed ridiculous until I thought how many Asians had been smuggled into the country by just such methods, hiding them in locked boxes stacked in Continental lorries.

The idea meant we should open another one, and quickly.

'It could be someone putting things in scratched theirselves because the screws stuck through inside, look.'

She pointed to the holes the screws had left inside the box.

I rubbed my finger along the stain to see if it was wet, but the soft wood absorbed like blotting-paper and it was impossible to tell whether the blood was wet and fresh, or whether the wood was damp because of something which had soaked in before.

It was then only three hours since Harry had loaded the boxes, though to me it felt like three days and—specially—nights.

I signalled her not to say any more and got to work with the chisel. It was as big a chisel as I had ever seen, so I did not stand on ceremony and slipped it behind the hasp of the next box to lever the screws right out of the soft wood.

That done I stood back a little, then kicked up under the lid as hard as I could. The lid went off backwards away from me.

She had the torch then and pointed it down into the box.

'Oh, no, no, no!' she cried suddenly, and went back from the box taking the light off the contents.

'Give me the torch!' I said, angrily.

I didn't want to see into the box, because the one flash I'd caught of the contents looked as bad as I had imagined, but I wanted to be sure.

As she handed over the light the beam swept the inside of the box, and I turned it away.

'Come out of here!' I said, taking her arm. 'Go ahead. Be careful—'

I added the last advice because in her hurry to get out of the truck she almost fell over the corner of one of the boxes.

We got out quickly into the grey light of the yard and she stopped, not knowing which way to go. The car was still in the gateway. I turned her towards the house.

'It's the only way,' I said.

We went back into the kitchen. I bolted the back door quite aware that I might be locking the enemy inside with us. We just had to hope we hadn't.

The place seemed ablaze with light after the gloom outside.

'We better see she's all right,' Anna said and took up a candle as she went out into the big room.

She wasn't going to talk about the boxes, as if, when she didn't mention them, they disappeared.

In any case, I didn't want to talk about them. There would be no point talking until I got in touch with the police, whenever that might happen, because I began to think the obvious reason for blocking our exits was to stop such a meeting taking place.

She waited for me by the big table. I held up a finger for silence and we both listened.

It was the quietest house I ever remembered. Dead quiet. Perhaps all the dust and rubbish swept into the many corners absorbed noise.

There was nothing to hear, not even the flutter of a candle. All the little flames were upright in the still air while we stood listening.

I began to hope we had locked the enemy out after all. He was out there because somebody had to have taken the lid off that one box, even if he did it from the inside.

Anna had suggested that someone had been inside it, pulling against my attempts to lift the lid. I didn't agree with that. I thought the lid wasn't a proper fit and had jammed itself at the corners.

'It is all right?' Anna watched me.

'I can't hear anything,' I said.

'Then we go to see?'

'All right.'

We went up the dreaded staircase. The candle flame flickered a little and our shadows walked up the walls all round us, giants, crookbacks, jerking, changing, shrinking down through the floor at the top.

I thought: She won't be there. She'll have vanished. She'll be there, but she'll be dead.

94

She'll be—

Anna opened the door, looked in, then entered the bedroom. I stood in the passage only too sharply aware of what was hidden by the door behind me.

'Are you all right, Arethusa?' I heard Anna say.

There was a sort of sleepy groan.

'I make you comfortable again. Lift your head. Lift—Ah, let me—There that's better.'

Anna came out again.

While waiting I had thought hard about what was best to do. It was necessary to wait only till daylight. The party outside would not try blockade then. People going to and fro along the road would turn their noses towards such a demonstration at Cob Weary, a place about which they were only too ready to think the worst.

And this time, whatever dreadful things they thought were not going to be right enough.

'Lock her in and take the key,' I said. 'It's the only door, isn't it?'

'I do not know that for sure. The cupboards are funny in this house. Some backs come open.'

'Just let me look,' I stepped towards the bedroom.

'No. She has just gone off. Don't wake her now, please.' She turned to the door. 'I lock it, as you say.'

I was not suspicious about anything any

more. I did not bother that she wouldn't let me go in the room. It just didn't matter, when one was surrounded by murdered bodies and blood oozed out of every crack in the floorboards.

At the time I had begun to think like that, because the only way to believe myself in such a situation as I was really in was to regard it as an interesting phenomenon which would vanish with daylight.

'What time does Harry come in the morning?' I said as we went down the stairs.

'He says about five, but I do not know for sure.'

It would not be light until after seven. Meanwhile Harry was going to walk into the truth about what he had been collecting in the lorry, unless I could stop him. It would be best if he didn't see it.

I thought that the people guarding the gate would not show themselves and let him come in. Once he was in he would be caught in the same bag as ourselves.

Then there would be no other outsider, they would have to fear, who might come to the house.

The cold thought shivered through me that they knew the time of daybreak as well as I did and would have to do their job before that happened. Whatever that job was.

I was reasonably sure that they were a mob who had come to take the profits the first mob had collected.

'We must wait,' I said. 'I'll make tea. Are there any biscuits?'

'Oh, I did not let you 'ave some dinner!' she said, as if recalling a disaster. 'I get you some breakfast. I do that.'

We went back into the kitchen. I was too worried and upset then to wonder about whether the frying pan was clean or not. She fried bacon and bread and made a pot of tea while I kept watch in the big room.

I remember that when the smell of the bacon drifted out from the kitchen I really began to feel I was waking from a night of fearful dreams. I wished the daylight would come and kill the whole thing; dissipate the corpses and wash out all the damned spots.

When I'd had a thick slice of fried bread smothered in bacon and drunk hot tea, a different feeling began to stir my thoughts.

Something had to be done about the fearful business. Somehow the police would have to be reached. The boxes in the truck had at last given something they could not regard as part of a rumour, as I had seen them loaded at Kingston and followed them back.

Of course, the whole problem of persuading the police was simple once they came as far as the tithe barn.

'You think you will fetch the coppers,' she said, watching me. ''Ow?'

The loss of the aspirate seemed to make the

question shoot out with a bang.

'I am thinking it out,' I said.

'But there is this car and this lorry stuck in the gates and nobody widdem, so what do you do? You do go by and then—poomp! Right on the bloody edd. I seen this 'appen before.'

'Here?'

'Oh, no, no. It was a customer. A wide boy, you know. They do this dead car business in his gate and when he go to get by—boomp! Right on the—'

'Bloody edd,' I ended for her. 'Yes. I have heard of it myself.'

I looked at her.

'At the front,' I said, 'we have a car but they have a lorry. One to them. But out at the back, we have a lorry and they have a car.'

Her eyes sparkled.

'You mean Bang?' she said, excitedly.

'Bang and bang again,' I said.

'But how do you start it?'

'There are some keys hanging on the dresser there. Vehicle keys.'

'Oh, yes, yes, yes.' she said, getting up. 'Harry puts them there. Yes, yes, yes. It will be fun!'

'Let's hope so,' I said. 'But sit down again. 'We have to be very careful. I'll tell you what we have to do.'

CHAPTER SEVEN

1

'Can we get into the barn without going near the gate where the car is?' I said.

'Yes, yes. There is a little door. But they did not see us before, did they?'

'I don't know. But if they see us go back there they'll guess what we're up to. We must have the benefit of surprise.'

Her eager expression changed abruptly.

'But what about 'er?' she said, and pointed in the air.

'She'll be all right. We're going to fetch the police, Anna.'

'That's what I mean! She won't like that. She don't like them nosing about.'

'But things have changed. This house is under siege.'

'No, it is all around not under. But she won't like the police more than that. I know, with her.'

I was not going to be held back by the wishes of the mad sleeper. If she had had a hand in several murders then it was time the police did look in on her. The way she was going on there would be a marked dent in the population within a year.

'We are going, Anna. We need the police.'

'Oh well, it is your foot you are putting in it.'

I began to realize there was something she had misunderstood.

'What did you think I meant when I said we must bust a way out?'

'To escape. I did not know anything about the police.'

'They've got to be called sooner or later. Now is the time.'

'You know I got a form,' she said, sulkily.

'What for?'

'For being sexy out of doors.'

'Oh, that's nothing.'

'They fine me plenty. I say what's the Common Market for then? But they make the fine just the same. Of course, I've given all that up, but they'll remember. It will spoil my reputation.'

'They won't bother with it at all, Anna. Don't worry about it. The one important thing is to get out of here and it's best to do it now. If we leave it too long Harry will turn up and walk right into trouble. You don't want that to happen, do you?'

'Poof to 'Arry,' she said, contemptuously.

'All right. You do. Now show me the way into the barn.' I took the little bunch of keys off the dresser. 'And we must be quiet!'

'Okay. Yes. You go out this side door round here, not out the back one.'

She led the way to the door. It was round a

corner past the great fireplace where the cooker was, so practically no light reached it from the candles.

I opened the door. It was quiet outside and still foggy. I could make out the roof line of the great barn against the lighter grey of the moonlit sky far above the fog. She closed the door and locked it before we went on.

She was very anxious about Mrs Browne not being disturbed.

We got into the barn by a 'small door' about five feet wide and eight high. Once inside we looked down the length of the barn to the truck at the end. The light, coming at that end through the huge double doors, was just enough for us to make our way down to the truck without falling over hay bales, boxes and other stuff lying around on the floor.

When we reached the front of the vehicle I stopped and signalled her for quiet. We listened, but there was nothing to be heard outside.

We climbed up into the cab and closed the doors by the latch handles to make no slamming noise. I put in the keys. I was relieved when one fitted. The starter was sluggish, so much so that it strained as if it would burst and my heart held off beating for a second or two. The battery had just enough oomph to do the job and the engine started.

I backed the vehicle out of the barn at a fast pace. The noise was incredible. I had forgotten the ramp was resting on the ground behind, and it clattered back over the brick yard as if the sky was raining dustbins. I swung the back almost up against the house wall, then crammed the gear in first and thundered off towards the gate.

The surprise was against us. The gate was empty. The car had gone.

We went on out.

'They gone! There is no need!' she shouted above the din from the back end.

'They're behind us!' I lied. 'I can see them in the mirror!'

We went crashing, clattering and banging on our way until my sensitive soul suggested we stop and fix the thing up. Before I could there was a challenging call from a police car behind.

I could have cheered as I pulled in to the side of the road and the police car passed and pulled in ahead.

'We 'ave got pinched,' she said. 'You 'ave mucked it up.'

I was down on the road when the sergeant came up. I saw him glance at the number plate and then at me.

'This vehicle is in a dangerous condition,' he said. 'The tailboard is drifting on the road.' He watched me for a moment. 'But this belongs to Cob, doesn't it? The farm there.'

He left out the other question which I could read in his face: 'Then what the hell are you doing driving it in this state in the middle of the night?'

'We were in a hurry to get to the police station,' I said. 'We were anxious in case we were followed.'

'Oh yes?' he said, with quiet interest.

Clearly he was still wondering what I was doing driving this clapped-out truck in the middle of a foggy night, with the tailboard down, etc.

'What business had you at the station, sir?' he said.

'If you look in the back, you'll see.'

He looked towards the back of the truck and then round to his car.

'Bring up a light, Tom,' he called.

His companion got out of the car and walked up with a big torch. It all seemed to be happening in slow motion.

The three of us went along to the back of the vehicle and the sergeant got up on to the ramp, with the torch in his hand and shone it into the body of the cattle wagon.

We heard him tramping in there and then he appeared on the ramp again.

'An empty box,' he said. 'Broken open, I should say.'

With some idiot feeling, I remembered we had come into the house after leaving the truck; Anna had insisted on seeing Mrs Browne, and then we had had a scratch meal, and in that time the boxes had been unloaded and probably taken away in the vehicles which had been blocking the gateways.

I clambered up the ramp and looked inside the body. It was, as the sergeant said, containing one empty box with the lid lying by it, just as I had seen it last.

'Well, sir?' the sergeant said. He sounded almost kindly.

I suspected the worst.

'There were five boxes in all,' I said.

'Do you mean they shook out on the road?' the sergeant said. 'Well, we came the same way, past Cob, and we haven't found any boxes in the road.'

He looked at me for a few seconds.

'I think the best thing is for us to give you a hand putting the back up and then I'll just take the details and make a report.'

We went down the ramp together. The back was duly pushed back up and fastened. The sergeant made notes.

'I might say, sir, that it isn't the first time we've had people running away from that place. It has a bad reputation.' He looked up and down the road. 'I think you'd best turn round and take this vehicle back. I see you have a member of the staff with you, so I'm sure it will be the best thing to do.'

'Thanks, Sergeant.'

He turned as if to go, and then looked back.

'What did you think was in the box, sir?'

I was sure he had heard all about dead bodies before, and I kept off that track.

'I thought it might be stolen property,' I said. I then told him who I was, and he then became interested.

'I see,' he said. 'Well, we've heard such a lot about the place that I've come to the point of believing none of it. It's just a madhouse. If you have some business there, I wish you the best of luck, but I don't think you'll get much change out of it.'

They helped me turn round and we parted. I drove slowly back.

'It was all tooken outs,' she said.

'Yes.'

'Perhaps that's what they comed for.'

'Quite likely.'

The fog was clearing. When we got back to Cob we could see the gateway and the front was clear. No lorry was blocking it.

2

We put the truck back in the barn then went into the house. We made more tea. I kept a watch out of the kitchen window for Harry to turn up with the idea of clearing the boxes out of the wagon.

The atmosphere of nightmare seemed worse after the weird disappearance of the incriminating coffins in the lumbering old vehicle. It was not quite so dreamlike after seeing the lorry at the front and the car at the back.

I had seen enough of the front block to be sure that the vehicle there had been a lorry and not a truck. Its flat sideless back had been the most prominent detail appearing through the fog. The only tall structure on it had been the cab, hardly visible by comparison with the tail.

So had they intended to carry away these mock-up coffins on the flat back of a lorry, lashed with rope or chain or whatever was carried so that anybody passing could see what was aboard? It seemed incredible, in view of the fact that sooner or later some police investigation was inevitable.

Whatever else happened in this place, when I had freed myself of it with enough evidence to carry conviction, I was going to make investigation certain.

We drank tea in the kitchen and she dozed off ... Mrs Browne's behaviour seemed to be the only way of getting any sort of angle on what was really going on.

The night she had come to Anna's cottage quite normal. A short time later we had come to the house and found her anything but normal.

The change might have been due to drink or drugs; the effect probably too quick for the first, but not for the second. Anyhow, she had been in a violent mood, accusing Harry, as if deserted by him, and then, as if losing all spirit, letting herself be taken up to bed, but not in her own room.

The earlier times when I had seen her, there had been two changes from one mood to another, and yet, as I remembered the scenes in detail, it did not seem that she might be mad. In each case, it had seemed to me to be deliberate, angry, getting rid of steam rather than letting her mind go rocketing off on its own.

Then why the anger? Why the fury in the solicitor's office when it seemed there would be long delay in settling the will?

It was then I had a twisted thought.

Was the husband dead?

People on gigantic fiddles sometimes arranged their own deaths by standing back while some other corpse filled the necessary bill.

In which case any delay in effecting probate of the will of the 'deceased' would naturally be nervously resented.

That could account for the verbal affray in the lawyer's office.

Again, supposing that Mrs Browne was being forced to carry out some part of the apparently late husband's business, and that part something she didn't like, her expressions of violent disapproval of a status she was forced to hold might well cause rapid changes of temperament.

A woman doing something evil on her own account wouldn't show signs of disapproval of her activities. One forced to do something she didn't like might well take to violent spasms in her behaviour. Taking it out on the farm hand, would be a way of putting it; or kicking the adulterer's horse might do better.

I was building up quite an interesting case for my own amusement, but when I came to thinking about a criminal letting his wife get away with a fortune under his bogus will I just couldn't fit that in.

Mrs Browne did not seem the kind of woman to let herself be forced to do something she hated and then share the proceeds with a forcer.

But this was all guesswork.

What wasn't guesswork was that the boxes had been taken from the barn, and one, at least, of the boxes had contained a dead man.

I couldn't help feeling that the rest of the boxes might have been filled with the same sort of thing.

But I couldn't imagine a woman renting a flat in order to receive dead bodies, then to bring them down to her own home in order that others might take them away.

Burke and Hare were long gone and I could not imagine any way that a collection of miscellaneous corpses could bring in commercial benefits.

I didn't believe cannibalism could suddenly have taken root in the community. Whatever else may be said about it, the idea is unattractive.

Then what else could there be? What other sort of handling could be commercially viable?

The more I thought of it, the more improbable the whole thing appeared.

I turned my mind to side incidents, such as the man who had attacked Anna. He had come out of the Hanging Room. Had he been some sort of investigator he would not have committed assault on one of the staff at the house. Nor would he have run as he had done.

The one motive he must have had was gain, probably from blackmail.

The number of people who were appearing as being in on the secret was astonishing.

In the first place, it seemed that the flat over the fish shop had been—amongst other places—a branch office where people brought their dead and paid Mrs Browne to take them away. She then brought them to Kent where, on the instant, almost, another mob with two vehicles, took them away somewhere else.

In order to allay any stories getting about, Mrs Browne—helped by any number of local gossips—had spread wild tales of bodies falling out of the walls, etc. The police had also been generously salted with these yarns; a useful device since it made them sceptical.

Once you had created a horror story people would laugh at it pleasurably, then, after a while, you'd be free to make it come true while people went on laughing.

Then came doubt. But was it really as easy

as that? At what point could you tell it was safe to go ahead? Carry out a local opinion survey?

I drank more tea. Whichever way I began to think about the Arethusa Greco-Browne problem the more tangled I got. I tried to comfort myself with words said to me once by a detective-inspector of great fame.

He had said: 'There is a simple solution to every mystery once you have pruned off the details which look as if they are important, but actually don't have anything to do with the main problem.'

I wondered what he would have cut out from this lot. Mrs Browne?

This time the thought came in a flash of sarcasm, but it was what I had thought before. It seemed I kept thinking it.

Was it possible that she might be floundering in the same sea of confusion and ignorance as I was?

Then a side question occurred. Why had I come to the point of having sympathy with the wretched woman?

Boxes were taken to a flat in Kingston, stored there, then carried away by Harry into Kent, where a gang picked them up. That would mean Cob Weary was merely being used as a staging post.

If she was the stooge in a long chain of transfer operations then she might well behave in flurries of passion from time to time.

Suppose that this body chain was operated

by her husband, then it was likely that it would be better for him to appear to be dead and become somebody else. By that means, payment to keep his wife quiet might neatly be done by making it over in a will.

Such an arrangement would account for her rage and impatience over clearance. She would be wanting to be paid and to get out before she was in sore trouble, and hesitation by the lawyers would mean only one thing to her— they were trying to find out if Browne had really died.

If also, the niece was in fact Browne's illegitimate daughter, then she might have gone to join him in his new life, wherever that was. It certainly wouldn't be in this country.

Everything was falling into place neatly. I might have been pleased except for the fact that it was pure guesswork and bore no relation to any person, living or dead.

I saw a figure crossing the yard and then somebody tried the back door. Finding it locked, the visitor banged on the door with what sounded like a mallet, but was, in fact, his fist.

Anna woke up at the noise.

'It's 'Arry,' she said, and bawled, 'Shut up, 'Arry!'

I opened the door. Harry stood outside a moment, staring at me, then he came in and looked round the kitchen.

'Where's missis?' he said.

'Asleep,' said Anna.

He looked towards the big room and across it to the stairs. All the doors were open. Some of the candles had burnt out but a few still shone and the light was quite good.

'She don't get too much of that,' he said. He picked up the teapot, lifted the lid and peered in. 'What's this? Piss?' He grunted then went to the sink and emptied the pot. He went to the cooker, put the pot on it, then pushed the heavy kettle on to the hot plate and started shovelling heaped spoonsful of tea into the pot.

It was a very odd scene because nobody spoke. It was as if we were each waiting for somebody else to talk and nobody would.

He made tea which looked like brown paint. Anna and I watched him, it seemed, minute after minute and still he didn't speak. It began to look as if Anna and I played a game of nerves on him, but he obviously knew it and played it back, as it were.

At last he spoke.

'Market's cancelled,' he said. 'Foot 'n mouth over Easenden. I wouldn't 'ave got up so smart 'fI'd known. Met Dyke in village. He told me.'

That explained why he sat there idly, only breaking his calm to slurp up the overkill tea.

Quite suddenly, he shoved his mug away from him across the table, got up and thumped out into the yard, of course, slamming the door behind him.

'Is he always like that in the morning?' I said.

'No. He is roughed up,' Anna said.

She almost fell asleep again. I waited. On cue I heard him stamp back across the yard.

He always slammed doors shut; this time he slammed it open to such effect that some whitish dust was shaken from the ceiling over it.

'They bin!' he shouted. 'You dint say!'

'Oo's bin?' Anna challenged.

'The buggers takes the boxes!'

'I don't know of buggers takin' boxers!' snapped Anna.

This jousting with the language could have baffled me had I not known beforehand what it all meant. I watched Harry while trying not to look too interested.

In his rage, Harry seemed to realize he had put his foot in it. I wondered if Harry usually gained something for the transfer of boxes and that was what was upsetting him.

'I was here all night,' I said. 'We had trouble. Somebody got in here. A burglar.'

'A burglar?' Harry said, staring. Then he laughed cynically. 'I wish 'im the best o' British luck. I do that!'

He turned and looked across the yard to the barn, then back.

'I got to get the cows,' he said, and thumped away, leaving the door wide open.

''Arry is good, really,' said Anna, 'but not

113

couth.'

'He knows the people who were here last night,' I said. 'And he didn't expect them till this morning.'

'They come because they knowed we was 'ere,' said Anna.

'How did they know unless they were already here?'

'That man 'oo ran out last night. Praps 'e told.'

'But that would mean he's one of them. If they weren't outside here then, he must have known where to find them to tell them.'

'But if they comed regular, why didn't she know 'im?'

'She didn't see him. He wasn't in the bedroom with you, was he?'

'No, no.'

'You mean that he got in here while she came down to the cottage to find us? That might be it.'

'Anything could be it. She never locks up nowhere, mostly, and sometimes I think she just give up hope.'

'Hope of what? Of keeping people out?'

'Of course. There are too many 'oles in this 'ouse. It's a crazy place.'

'We kept it locked.'

'We did not see 'oo was in first. Wiv no bloody lights this is what 'appens.'

CHAPTER EIGHT

1

'Why did she come down to the cottage and find us?' I said.

'I am trying to guess. But she changed her mind when she opened my door. I could see on her face.' Anna frowned. 'Praps she was upset seeing you was there.'

'Possibly. But why? If she'd been suspicious she would have come in and tried to find out what we were up to,' I said. 'She knew we were both in there, because it was her car which was waiting out in the lane. But when she opened the door—'

'She lost her guts,' Anna ended for me.

'Courage,' I amended.

'You say it different to Arry.'

'*From* Arry—' my correction ended in trapping myself.

'What from Arry?' she said curiously.

'Nothing!'

She stared moodily at the candles on the table.

'I must go to see she is all right.' She got up, and this time walked out of the kitchen and across the big room without bothering about my company for bodyguard.

115

That was a curious change in her behaviour, as if she had decided she need no longer fear the Black Upstairs.

Or perhaps her fear was overcome by her need to go alone, no matter what happened.

It was a grand night for guessing. As there was no secure bit of evidence to which one might hitch a speculation, one might as well cast one's guesses on the water and hope to recognize them again later.

How does one trade in dead bodies so that the profits make it worthwhile taking grave risks? Not even my flights of lugubrious imagination could light on a single means of getting rich in such an industry.

Then *were* they bodies? If not, what were they?

My views of the contents of the room and of the box in the van had been of the briefest and in distorted light. Neither a candle, flickering, nor a torch flashing across the object gives more than a short, shocking nightmare vision. In both cases my mind was in a dark, fearful mood, half expecting horror, and perhaps had filled in details in my vision which I had not, in fact, seen.

It would be best, I decided, to take another look in that room by a steadier light. Anna had taken my torch. I did not fancy using a candle again even for a long steady look at the hanging men. In my heart, I didn't want to look at all, but somehow I had to straighten out my mind.

I got up from my chair. The kitchen door opened again. Harry marched in leaving the door to fall to behind him. He glared at me as he approached, and then sat down in a chair across the table from me.

'I wants words,' he said.

I sat down facing him.

'Okay. Say what you have in mind.'

'You're to do with law,' he said, 'and could be but there's some needed around here.'

I was surprised but tried not to show it.

'What do you mean, Harry?'

'I'm not sure for sure,' he said, frowning, 'but them fellers what takes the boxes shouldn't 'ave come in the middle of the night. They could have been burglars, like. Mistook for. I di'n't expect them in the middle of the night. Are you sure they was the right fellers?'

'I didn't see them,' I said. 'And if I had I wouldn't know whether they were regular or not.'

'They don't come regler,' he said. ''Tis just now and again when I haves boxes to collect. They comes next morning, not in the middle of the bloody night.'

'There was a lorry and a car,' I said. 'That's all I know.'

'State car?'

'Yes, it was an estate car.'

'What's a lorry for, then?'

'What do they usually bring?'

'Big state car. That's all. Big enough. What's this lorry for?'

He frowned at me as if the mystery of the lorry was something to do with my activities. I thought I had better tell him what it had been used for and see what his reaction was. I told him.

His brows almost covered his bulging eyeballs his frown was so intense.

'Block the gate?' he said. 'What bloody for?'

'So I couldn't get away and tell the police, I suppose.'

'But why wouldn't they like the pleece telled? What's the matter with telling them? It's oney boxes er books, innit? Never worried about pleece before.'

It was becoming clear that Harry, and probably a lot of others, were being played for suckers, for if anything did bring the police into this affair, the suckers would be the first for the chop, while the others, being at a distance, would probably get clear.

I watched Harry trying to work things out. He thought he had carted boxes of books. The lids had been locked so he had never seen inside a box. He was just the porter.

At last he looked up from glaring at the table top.

'It was books, weren't it? I mean, it weren't drugs or nothen like that, eh?' Then he sat back, slightly relieved. 'Porn!' he said, and pointed at me. 'That's it! Porn books. Them what the pleece takes for magistrates ter read. All bums and that.' He snapped his mighty fingers. 'I been took for a sucker! That's what. That's why they drop me a quid each time they picks up the boxes! Porn! Gaw!'

He got up and walked out to the cows again, moving as if in a dream. He had found a solution good enough for him.

But as he got outside and slammed the door, I heard him shout.

'Hey! What're'y doin'?'

I got up and looked through the window to the yard. A man with a shotgun under his arm was standing by the barn doors looking at Harry, whose back was to me. When I saw that gun I didn't think the fellow was after rabbits.

'Get the cows out,' the man said.

'Well, er course I'll get bloody cows out! What're you telling about? What do you want?'

'I'll tell yer when you've finished 'em off. Get on with it!' He signalled where Harry was to go with the gun barrel.

For a moment I feared that Harry would object and rush at him, only to get a bellyful of shot. He did look for a few dreadful seconds as if he would, but then, obviously, he put his cows first and stamped away.

When he went out of sight, the gunman turned his head and looked towards the house. For a moment we looked at each other. He broke his gun, ensured that both barrels were loaded, and then closed it and looked to me again.

Anna came back into the kitchen behind me. I turned from the window.

'I don't find her,' she said, shortly. It sounded an annoyed tone.

An uneasy sick feeling struck the pit of my stomach.

'Did you look in the other rooms?'

'No! I don't look in any other rooms up there. Arry said the wallpaper is yooman skins!'

'Harry pulls your leg a bit,' I said.

'He don't get near my legs unless I say!'

'It's an expression,' I said. 'Was the bed quite empty?'

'Of course, she was not there!'

'What about your coat? Was that there?'

'No. I spect she was cold.'

'Whose room is that?'

'It is a spare. She wouldn't go in her room.'

'Why not?'

'I don't ask to argue. I just say okay.'

'There's a man out in the yard. Look. Do you know him?'

She stared, her head on one side.

'What's he got a gun like that for?'

'He's going out shooting, I expect. Do you know him?'

'I think I do, but I think I don't. When I think I do he don't look like that, as if he is not supposed to look like that. Do you know what I mean to say?'

'You seem to know him but there's something strange about him?'

'Yes! That is right. I know him but he is not like that.'

'Can you say what is different about him?'

'Yes, yes. Now I know. He is dressed funny to what I see him in before. Before he has long black coat and collar to cut his neck upwards like, and also he has the hat like a basin.'

'A bowler. Where did you see him?'

'In Kingston.'

'Did he look like a man at a funeral?'

'Yes, yes! That is what he looks when they stand at the grave and look sad.'

'You saw him in the flat at Kingston?'

'Yes. He haves two bloody foreigners with him as well.'

She went to the door. I grabbed her arm.

'Where are you going?' I said.

'I tell him to piss off,' she said, surprised.

'Leave him alone. He's in a bad temper. And he's waiting for a friend.'

'Then he can wait out in the bloody road.' She grabbed the latch.

I pulled her away from the door.

'Leave him alone, Anna, and don't use Harry's talk. It's not elegant.'

'But I will tell him—'

'We ought to find out where Mrs Browne went.'

'I am not looking into the rooms up there.

They gives Arry the wets.'

'Anna! Which is the room she usually uses?'

'The one next to that one what she ad.'

'Let's look in there.' I turned to go to the big room.

She pulled me back, then turned and pointed at the window as if taking aim with a pistol.

'I seen im,' she said, 'upstairs as well!'

'When?'

'Weeks ago. But when he turn his face then I remember he looked just like that in her room.'

'What was he doing there? Do you know?'

'No. I tell er and she says, "I get rid of the sneaky sod" and she go up and I don't see him any more.'

'What was he wearing then?'

'Like a work man. All rough and dirty. He is different every time.'

'It's a very expensive gun he's got,' I said. 'Let us go and find Mrs Browne.'

2

As we went out I turned back and could still see the man with the gun standing in that grey light of dawn and taking his guard very seriously.

It was an unpleasant puzzle I was trying to work out as we crossed the big room. As the gang had already taken the boxes, why had they come back? Or were they the same gang as had taken the boxes? Were we likely to find ourselves in the middle of a gang war?

One thing was certain. We were in the middle of something very unpleasant, and it could have an even more unpleasant kind of ending.

Walking towards the stairs with Anna I felt like cursing the pop-eyed solicitors who had ever thought of this clever plan.

Upstairs we looked into the room where Anna had left Mrs Browne; it was empty. We looked into the one I had searched and found the odd clothing in the cupboards. That, too, was empty.

Anna began to shout.

'Arethusa! Mrs B! Arethusie! Arry! Where you bloody iding?'

There was no answer.

The light was grey but at least, we could see by it as it filtered through the dirty windows in the passage. The scene it showed was not inviting but it wasn't so daunting as it had been by candlelight.

We went along to the Guest Room. My imagination was by then so warped by the night's events that my stomach quailed at the door and I stood for a moment, looking at the hefty oak panels.

'Look in,' Anna said. 'She might be asleep, praps.'

I opened the door. There were four small

windows on the far wall, beginning to glow with the gloom of a new grey dawn.

'Is she there?'

I went in and looked round. She came close behind me. As soon as I sensed her right at my back I knew we had made an error.

'Back!' I said. 'Outside—'

As I turned and shoved her towards the door, it slammed shut and I heard a steel peg being plugged in to lock the latch on the outside.

'There!' I said, and turned her aside as I came to the door and tried the latch, just to make sure. It was fixed solid.

'Arethusie!' Anna yelled. 'Don't joke on me! Open the bloody door! Arry!'

'Shut up, Anna!'

She stopped suddenly and looked round at me in surprise.

I couldn't tell her that her half-hysterical screaming was very bad for my already suffering nerves, so I signalled for silence with a warning finger and crossed the room to the windows.

They were very small and stuck fast by years of neglect. In any case they were too small to get out of. I turned back and looked across at the bed. It was covered in a sheet and looked like a ghost bed in the gloom. Anna was clutching my torch like a club.

'Bring the light here,' I said.

She came across to me and handed over the

torch. To my relief it still worked. As I was then thinking the worst of the whole situation I fancied she might have hit something with it and burst the bulb.

I began to search the cupboards, opening each door with care and a foot against the bottom of the door in case something tried to push it open by falling out of the cupboard.

There seemed to be nothing but a few old heavy curtains hiding away in the three cupboards, and that made a sickening thought enter my mind.

What happened to The Thing which had made Harry stop his cleaning operations? Surely he had not cleared it away? He did not seem the sort to refuse so definitely and then agree later.

But, of course, there could be numbers of people coming and going in this place, and since it appeared to be an exchange market for cadavers, perhaps it had been removed in the course of business.

Anna was curiously silent during my search, and spoke only when I'd finished.

'Why 'ave she done it?' Anna said, blankly.

'I don't think she did it,' I said.

'You mean that man with the gun? What 'ave we got to do with 'im?'

'I don't know, but he does,' I said.

'Are we going to get hurt?' she said, watching me.

'I hope not,' I said. 'I hope that locking us in

125

here is a sign they just want to get us out of the way till they've gone.'

She came to me.

'Cuddle me,' she said, in a funny little voice. 'I am shattered wiv fright.'

I put my arm round her and we stood awhile together, with me trying to think of a way to get out of the room.

There had been a lot of talk about false backs to cupboards and trapdoors in walls. Such are easily talked about, not so easy to find, but I decided to look after Anna had finished shivering.

The house was as quiet as ever. If anything was going on in it, then the action was practically silent.

Now and again the quiet was broken by the soft sound of a vehicle passing on the road, but the stuck windows made the noise seem distant.

'I am better,' Anna said. 'Now we can smash the bloody door down.'

'That's not the best way, Anna. We'll find a way where they won't hear us.'

I went and looked out of the window. It was a grey morning outside. I saw a car go by in the road and that was the only sign of life out there. There were no guards on the gate, no blocking vehicles, nothing at all.

The man with the shotgun had probably turned up as part of a gang who intended to take away some more goods and wanted us out

126

of the way while they did it.

But Harry was around somewhere down there. It seemed to me that he and the gunman had known each other, or he wouldn't have gone on to his cows quite as he had done.

Perhaps he hadn't been locked up, in which case he might—

I decided not to indulge in aimless optimism, but get on with trying to find a way out of the room, according to legend.

At the time I was sorely scared by the thought of what might happen to us sooner or later. If their business was indeed the handling of cadavers, they would not hesitate to obtain a couple more.

In fact this was a situation where two murders could be carried out merely as part of a business transaction.

I began to search the sides and back of the first cupboard. Some of the old joints in the wood had widened with age and settlement of the building so it was difficult to make out if any joint was wider than it needed to be.

In the process of search I pushed and tapped and tried to slide panels. I was somewhat distracted by her urgent whispers, asking me if I'd found it, and was I going to be much longer?

By the time I started to explore the third cupboard my hopes had sunk to the spiritual bottom.

Then I applied a little commonsense to the

problem. Why were the insides of the cupboards boarded? Cupboards in walls, I thought, were mostly plastered all round back and sides, therefore the boarding might have been done to hide the fact that one cupboard back was not a cupboard back.

I went at the third cupboard with greater care, and found the false back by tripping on the old curtains and knocking my head against the back wall.

When I looked there was a two-inch gap down one side of the cupboard back. I slid it to one side, and the legend became exhilarating truth.

But exhilaration was brief. The cupboard only led into another cupboard.

'Can we get out?' she hissed from outside my box of discovery.

'We can get into another cupboard,' I said glumly. 'It's just a hiding place.'

She used some Harry language. I didn't object but rather agreed. But then I wondered if my feelings were in too dampened a mood to go on hoping and I looked at the back of the second cupboard.

There was a crack down the middle of it, because the whole back was made of two wide planks of wood.

Then I realized that so were the doors of the Guest Room cupboards and I shone the torch all round the edges to find a catch and there wasn't one.

I put my hand flat on the left-hand plank and it gave a little but didn't open. Then I realized it might be the hinge side and pushed the opposite edge. The door grunted and pushed open. I looked into the bedroom next door.

So one legend at least was true about this place. There was a go-through cupboard.

She came crowding in behind me. I thought that if I ever wanted a limpet assistant, she would make a good one.

We stepped through into the other bedroom and stopped when we saw a woman sitting on the bed with her face buried in her hands. Her back was towards us and she didn't seem to have heard us.

'It's *err*!' Anna whispered close to my ear. 'What we do?'

I held a hand up to Anna to stay where she was and walked round the bottom of the bed.

'Mrs Browne,' I said quietly.

The woman stayed in that curiously bent position. I touched her shoulder.

'Mrs Browne—'

She collapsed slowly, very slowly, so that it was difficult to believe she was actually falling. I went forward and got my hands to her shoulders to stop her going sideways to the floor.

I made her go slightly back so that she would fall along the bed. She went over sideways to the bed and just lay there.

It looked as if she was dead.

CHAPTER NINE

1

'She ain't gone, ave she?'

I found the dull dread of the discovery almost made into the ridiculous by the extraordinary words from the beautiful Alsatian woman.

'I don't know,' I said.

Anna passed me and bent down beside the bed.

'Arethusa,' she said huskily. 'Come on, now, you snap out of it, bloody well!'

I could see that for a moment Anna thought the same as I, that Mrs Browne was dead. Then Anna stood up.

'You got a weak belly, you look the other way,' she said. 'You don't elp anyway. I try myself.'

I went and looked out of the window at the grey day. The noises of the resuscitation attempt were awful to hear. It sounded like somebody opening and closing a rusty pair of bellows together with coughs, spits, grunts, thumps and poomphs.

Then Anna gasped and drew in a great breath.

'She comes, she is okay!'

I looked round. Mrs Browne looked a lifeless body stretched out on the bed and covered with a blanket, but as I bent closer I saw she was breathing.

'What happened to her?' I said.

'I would think she runned out of breff. What do you call it?'

'Asphyxiation. Do you mean somebody choked her?'

'With a pillow, praps? Maybe. I don't know. I would have to be a doctor to know. Do they go blue in the face?'

'I don't know either, but I have heard something like that. What I really meant was, do you think she was attacked? She was sitting up on the bed when we found her. Could she have sat up if she had been nearly killed?'

'I don't know, but she did not breeve when I started on her, and her heart did not beat, either because I felt her polse, and it was not.'

I looked round the room, then went and lifted the end of the blanket off Mrs Browne's neck, but I could see no bruises which she would have had if somebody had tried to choke her by hand. Perhaps the pillow idea was best. Smothered while still sleeping, and a drugged sleep at that, might have meant no struggle for life at all.

But how had she got into this room? The answer was there might be more backless cupboards, or the door.

I went to the door. It was locked, but the locking peg on its chain was on the inside. I pulled it out and the latch lifted normally.

Again I looked round the room. The woman had been in no fit state to have put that small peg into its hole in the door.

It looked as if someone had brought the woman into this room, smothered her and had then got out through some backless cupboard. But I was worried as to how Mrs Browne could have been sitting up on her own after a smothering attack, and why a pillow had not been lying on the bed rumpled up, as surely one must have been if such a method had been used.

I didn't think too long about that mystery because now I knew we could walk out, it was necessary first to work out what should be done when I did.

Or, looking at Anna and the way she was watching me, I should have thought, 'when *we* did'. It did not seem to me that I would be able to lose my limpet assistant without tying her to a piece of heavy furniture.

'I'd better take a look first,' I said. 'Stay with her while I find out who's here.'

'You come back!' she hissed.

'Of course.'

I stepped out into the passage. The place was quiet as a tomb, which I already thought it was. I went to the top of the stairs and listened, but heard nothing or anyone about the place.

My going down the stairs was the quietest I had ever managed. The silence was too heavy to risk making a noise in.

The big room was empty. I went quickly to the kitchen, and nobody was there either. I went back and looked along the hallway to the front door. It was open. I saw my car standing out there all alone in the grey day.

It was an invitation to run and get out of the place, but either honour or guilt made me go back upstairs.

'They've gone,' I said. 'There's nobody here. We must get out quickly!'

'No!'

I swung back to Anna unable to believe my ears.

'You don't want to go?'

'I mean she is ill. We must take her to the nursing home! Then we can go.'

'What nursing home?'

'It is about three miles. She ave been there before. I show you. We get her out first.'

I hesitated. If any of the enemy came back while we were struggling to get an unconscious woman down to the car, we should all be sunk. But it was true we couldn't leave her in the state she was in then.

'All right. Get her wrapped up. It'll be cold outside. I'll just make sure everything's clear.'

I went out again and closed the door behind me. Once more I listened, but heard only muffled sounds from inside the bedroom. I crossed the passage and stopped at the door of the death room. I think I hesitated for some seconds before trying the handle, for this door was the only one around with a modern lock alongside the traditional latch.

The door pushed in easily and without making a sound. I kept my eyes on the back of the door as long as I could, and at last got courage enough to look at the grisly scene in the light of day.

The room was empty. My life is anticlimax upon flop upon kerdunk.

I walked into a bare, empty room, with no basins on the floor. But there were hooks screwed into the ceiling beams; the sort of things one finds in old kitchens for hanging hams, cheeses of sweating cream, and other fancies.

But I had not dreamt anything. The room had been cleared out as part of the evacuation.

Back in the bedroom I saw that Anna had bundled the unconscious woman up pretty well, but there was the problem that she was as flaccid as a bag of flour. She was also a very big woman, perhaps about sixteen stone. I doubted if I could get her downstairs with a fireman's lift.

'I take her by the knees and you get her shoulders and then she won't bend too much, praps.'

'We'll have to try.'

It was quite difficult. Every time Anna came too close to me the woman sagged and almost hit the floor, and when we pulled apart one or the other of us nearly let go altogether. It was probably the clumsiest piece of first-aid transport ever devised, but we did get her to the car and into the back seat.

Anna showed me the way.

'It's a big ouse in the country all by itself,' she said. 'I show you when we get there.'

I started the engine, and then remembered Harry. I didn't say anything then, but when we got out of the gate I turned right and right again down the lane past the barn and the gate which the car had blocked.

'You know the way then?' Anna said.

'No. I want to know what happened to Arry—Harry,' I corrected myself and thought that if I was with this girl much longer I would never be able to say Harry again.

I stopped by the gate and went on foot to look for him. He wasn't in the barn. I found him in a shed sitting in a wheelbarrow and staring out of the open door. He looked up at me but didn't get up.

'Has that man gone? The one with the shotgun?'

'Wesson? Yes, he's gorn. Never stays long. He knows one of these ard days I'll blow is bloody edd orff.'

'Where does he come from?'

'Ask missis. I donno.'

'He comes here often?'

'When they has business. They talks business, his boss and err. To do with they boxes. I don't reckon as that's farm work, they boxes. Some side-line she's got. That niece praps. She had to do with it when she was about. Not that she was ere long. In and out like a horse's—' He added some proof of veterinary knowledge with which I will not bother.

'We're taking Mrs Browne to hospital. She's not well.'

'Poor old cow,' Harry said. 'Mark you, if she took a bit more care where she'm goin' I reckon as she'd feel better.'

With that he got up out of the wheelbarrow and just walked out of the shed. I walked back to the car, and we drove on to find the nursing home.

It was an old country house in extensive grounds walled all round. The house and grounds were still well kept which suggested that the fees at this home were of the very highest.

We pulled up at the grand front entrance. There were two cars parked just beyond the entrance, both facing us.

As I got out to make our purpose known to reception I walked past the cars and I saw that one of them was of the same type which had blocked the gateway at Cob Weary in the night.

I spoke to a middle-aged woman at the

reception counter, smartly dressed in white overall. I explained why I was there.

'Mrs Greco-Browne!' the woman said, with a curious expression. 'Yes, of course. She is a patient of ours. She is in the car?'

'She needs immediate attention,' I said. 'She is practically unconscious.'

'Oh.' She pressed a bell. 'I'll get the porters out with a stretcher.' She gave the order on a telephone, then began to fill in a form. 'I shall have to have an authority to have her here for treatment. Are you a friend?'

'In fact I am a representative of her solicitors.'

'Oh, that will do, I'm sure. If you just sign—' she turned the form towards me and pushed it across the counter to me, '—there.'

I signed, then turned to look out of the doorway to see two porters with a stretcher on a trolley going towards my car. They were very quick and efficient. It was not until they had been wheeled into the hospital and out of sight that I saw an orderly in a white coat coming down the corridor towards me.

He stopped, knocked on a door and went in.

I had seen him before.

He was the man called Wesson.

I went out to Anna pretty quickly.

'Are you sure this was the place she came to before?' I said.

'Sure, sure. She is friendly wid dem. It is all right.'

She looked anxiously at me as if unhappy about my doubts.

I didn't know enough about Mrs Browne's affairs or those of her business colleagues to justify my feelings about her safety at the hospital. I drove slowly away, my head buzzing with unhappy thoughts and alarms.

2

'Where you goin'?' she said.

'To London and the solicitors.'

'That's no good! They are a lot of crooked buggers.'

'Anna, they are very reliable people. They will help you.'

'I don't want no bloody elp.'

'We are going to London!'

'Then I must get my tings. You take me to my ouse and get my tings.'

'All right.'

Turning down through the narrow lane which ran past her cottage and on to the corner at Cob, I noticed a car some distance behind us. It looked to me like the one I had seen outside the nursing home, and the one I thought I had seen jamming the farm gate at Cob.

I had the feeling we were not going to get to London and the solicitors. To try and run on ahead of the follower might be successful, but only for a while. They would catch up when they really meant to.

With sight of that nursing home the idea, faint before, that we might be up against an organization, became quite vivid.

I turned into the little piece of ground fronting the cottage. No car passed the opening after we stopped, so it seemed the follower was playing a stalking game.

'You come in,' Anna said.

'What for?'

'To carry. I got a lot of bloody stuff to carry.'

'Wait a minute! You're not taking everything, are you?'

'I am moving into your ouse, like you said.'

'But, Anna, I didn't say!'

'Don't you worry. I cook good.'

She went into the cottage. After a look back at the apparently empty lane, I went in after her.

'Anna, we're being followed.'

Half way across the room she stopped and looked back.

'You sure?'

'Someone from the nursing home who was at Cob last night with a gun.'

She came out with a sudden, sharp Harryism.

'I thought you would make a bugger of it!' she said, and then changed her mind. 'Oh no I don't! I am sorry to say that,' and she flung her arms round my neck and kissed me. 'You forgive? I do not care if they follow. You will defend my honour and I will kick him in the eye.'

She let go.

'Do we go out and sock im now?' she said.

'No, Anna. That isn't the idea at all,' I said. 'What we shall do now is go into the village and I shall make a phone call from the pub there.'

She stiffened and pointed at my face.

'You do not call the police!'

'At the moment I have nothing to call the police about,' I said.

That remark was true, because, in this Cob Weary affair, every time I saw any definite evidence that might be worked on, it was stolen while my back was turned. At that time I had virtually nothing but memory to offer as evidence of evil.

And even that evidence was uncertain, because I didn't know if the corpses were those of murdered people, or whether there was just a trade in dead people.

And at that moment I did not know where I could put my finger on a corpse to corroborate my suspicions.

Worst of all were the apparent details of the gory business, which no one would accept as true without gory exhibits to substantiate such a rigmarole.

We went to the pub which had just opened

its doors to the public. I ordered drinks and asked if I might use one of the phones.

'Take your pick,' the innkeeper said proudly. 'If you wants privacy there's a genuine restored oak phone box with leather doorstrap just outside the back door. I'll show you.'

He showed me out of the back door into what was a beer garden, iron furniture stacked up in a summerhouse for the winter. I used the box to get in touch with Miss Jansen at the solicitors.

'I've had to take Mrs Greco-Browne to a nursing home,' I said and gave the details. 'Do you know anything about this place? It's called Hills House, on the Sussex border a couple of miles up from Northam.'

She gave instructions to somebody with her to find out, and spoke to me again, asking what I'd found, if anything.

When I told her what I'd seen and how the evidence had been removed, piece by piece, body by body she was quiet for a few seconds after I'd finished.

'Do you believe me?' I said, surprised.

'Well, it's possible,' she said slowly. 'I have heard one or two stories drifting about in the wind that might account for what you've seen, but I doubt whether it means murder.'

'What do you mean? Grave robbing?'

'No—Oh, thank you, Mary. Hang on, Mr Keyes. Your hospital has arrived . . .' There was a pause, then, 'It is a very private nursing home. The sort of place where families who don't have a lot of sentiment, send their unwanted relatives to live and be cared for. There is quite a market for that, you know. In this case there is a resident doctor, a surgeon of the Royal College; Mr George Padella— Hang on again. I'll be back.'

I heard activity at the other end of the line, then she came back, her voice sharper.

'A doctor of this name was staying at Nice when Greco-Browne died. He was called to help, and went, but said the man was dead and they would have to get a local man to attend and certify. That's interesting.'

'I don't think he's dead,' I said.

'That's even more interesting,' Miss Jansen said. 'Tell me more of what you think.'

I told her. It seemed to make her very thoughtful.

'You're doing well, Mr Keyes. I'm not sure what's best to do now. It does look as if Mrs Greco-Browne has been taken back into the protection of the conspirators, if this connection between Padella and her husband is right.'

Yes, I thought; that is just what it does look like, and it was Anna who had suggested it, just as if it was not hospital treatment that mattered so much as getting Arethusa into the protection of the conspiracy.

When I rang off, I stood a minute or two thinking about Anna. Right from the start she

142

had stuck to me like a limpet, as I had remarked before, so that she had known what I was doing all the time while herself playing the part of cheerful, but concerned innocence.

Had I been conned almost constantly during this short visit to Cob Weary?

When I went back to find her in the bar, she had gone.

CHAPTER TEN

1

'What happened to the lady?' I said, stopping as I went into the bar.

'She went out there, thumbed a lift and went,' the landlord said.

'Which way?'

'Where she come from—Cob.'

I drank some beer, then thanked him and went out. I drove fairly fast back to the tumbledown charnel house, then left the car out in the road and walked down the lane to the farm gate. I kept on the grass verge to make as little noise as possible. When I reached the gate I heard voices or rather, one voice.

'I say you come or they blow your bloody edd orff!' Anna said, furiously. 'If you stay ere you get your frote cut out! They are a bad lot.'

'They got to be bad to blow me edd orff,' shouted Harry, 'but if they cut me bloody frote as well they got to be daft!'

'Don't you be funny or I smack your bum!' she threatened improbably.

'Look, I growed up last week,' Harry said. ''Aven't you bloody noticed yet? If there's any smacken done it's gonna be me smacken all the others around, mark me. If they comed ere blowing and cutten I'll smack their bloody edds off you take it from me, Annie.'

'Don't be so silly, there's fousands of 'em, all in white coats and carry out away on a cart with a stretcher on it. I seed it all this morning.'

Harry's note changed. It became sharper.

'What're you talken about?'

'It's a orspittle!' she said. 'We took er down there and it was the lot that comes ere and takes the boxes you bring—'

'Steady a minute—steady—steady!' Harry said firmly. 'Are you sure? Medicals and that?'

'Doctors.'

'It was a doctor supposed to be ere oncet,' he said, quite slowly. 'And them bodies fallen out the walls. Them as I saw weren't bodies, Annie. Bloody imitations, they was and all orrible. Make you sick they did. What the flamen ell anybody wants with things around like that I don't know. I don't think she did. You see, she won't touch 'em either. When I come down that day when I found one up in the bedroom, she got round me after to take it

144

away for er. I get sorry for er, Annie. Then I do what she wants, and she cries. I don't like that, but I reckon she don't like all this any more than I do.'

I went into the bar where they were. Both looked round.

'If she came to get you to leave here, Harry, I think she's right. It's a bad lot that comes here for the boxes and I think they may want to keep you quiet.'

'Leave ere?' he said, frowning terribly. 'Leave me cows? But oo'll look after 'em? You can't just leave cows like that! Not like that, you can't!'

I could see he wouldn't be moved from his minding, yet he had to be got out of that place, because, like Anna, I was almost certain the men would come and get at such a valuable witness as he obviously was.

Until they saw me that morning turning up at the nursing home, they may have felt that their screen was safe, but seeing me with Mrs Browne, who, perhaps, was supposed to be dead in Cob Weary after suffocating, must have caused an instant discussion.

My view then was that as I had taken her there and signed the acceptance form they would not attempt to blot her out again. After all, she was safe and silent in their hands. Harry was still out in the open and he knew those dealers in strange boxes by sight.

'Is there a field near where you live where

you can take the cows in for a day or two?' I said.

'Old Rabble's you mean? Yeh, e would but e'd charge, that one. E'd charge fine.'

'I'll pay that,' I said. 'Which way is it?'

'I can't get 'em all in the truck?' he said angrily. 'Taint that big!'

'Which way is it?'

'Down lane ere, turn left at bottom. Bout mile an arf.'

'Drive 'em,' I said.

'Caw!' he laughed. 'Right wayward lot er buggers they is to drive, I tell yer!'

'The stragglier the better,' I said. 'You bring 'em out. I'll follow in the car. We can keep 'em going like that.'

'You ever done it afore?' he said curiously.

'Of course.' There was no point in telling truths at a time like that. As soon as the cows were in the lane, anyone coming up it would have to back down again, as the width was hardly enough for cow and car. With fourteen cows in between a follower and Harry, and me behind, the only thing for a silencing agent to do would be to get back out of it.

Anna came with me round to the car and we drove into the lane to stop the cows turning the wrong way.

They came out with a certain rumbling, grumbling noise and looks of baleful annoyance at being disturbed. They were Herefords. One thing I know about Herefords

146

is that the bulls are almost gentle because the cows are very rough when they feel like it.

Harry came out and closed the gate. He had a stick and prodded here and there and made terrifying noises which failed to impress the big animals. Since there was only one way they could go they started down the lane, spreading out as much as they could to sample the hedges.

In the distance ahead a car came round the bend in the lane, but saw the obstruction and stopped. The lane looked like a sea of uncontrolled cattle which had complete control of the right of way. I recognized the car as the one which had stood beside our gate-jammer at the nursing home.

It started to back and disappeared round the bend.

It looked as if the plan was working. Harry was being protected by those he spent his time protesting.

'It was them buggers,' Anne said, pointing through the windscreen.

'You really must stop all this rural language, Anna,' I said. 'It sounds absurd from such a beautiful girl.'

'Oh, you think I am beautiful, yes? That is good. Now I will come to your ouse and make you very appy. But it was them. I seen that car at that home place.'

'I know.'

Progress was very slow. The hedge sampling

was spreading despite Harry's shouts, yells, threats and curses. I think he was trying to imitate the voice of an angry bull.

I wondered why the men in the car had waited so long before coming back to Cob. It seemed to indicate an uncertainty about what was best to do. That idea pleased me. It was, in fact, the first idea which had pleased me since I had come to this forsaken place.

The lane came to a junction just round the bend and some cows went one way, some another and some just stayed in the middle of the junction and dropped various tributes to the energetic attempts of Harry to get them all down the left-hand lane.

At this point, as we waited, I kept a very sharp eye open all round but did not spot the prowling car in either branch of the lane. I also looked behind, for I assumed it was possible to beat around the lanes and come up behind us. There was nothing to be seen behind.

We got the cows to the gate of Rabble's field, and Harry drove them in. At first there was some protesting, but when it was noticed the grass was good inside, they all lumbered in.

I shouted out of the window as Harry shut the gate.

'Wipe your feet on the grass and then get in,' I said.

He was wiping his feet by the side of the car when I saw the following car appear in my mirror.

'Get in!' I shouted.

Harry looked surprised. Anna flung her door open, grabbed his arm and tugged him so he fell in on top of her and almost on top of me as well. I started off. He yelled when the door slammed against his foot.

'Shut up! Get yourself in! They're right behind!'

They managed to sort themselves out but almost toppled on me twice as I sped along that winding lane with the trailing car close up behind.

'Where you going to go?' Anna shouted, as if I was deaf.

'To the police station!'

'No! You let me out!' she cried, trying to open the door past Harry's bulk.

'Hold her down, Harry! I'm trying to save the lot of us!'

'Old still, you soppy cow!' Harry said grabbing her.

'You call me a cow like them?' she shouted, forgetting her fear of the police. 'You call me cows? I beat you—!'

'Keep still!' I shouted, as she almost got mixed in with the wheel. 'Hold her, Harry! Hold her!'

There was no room for play in those lanes and with a fast moving car right up our tail. From the ferocity of their following now I realized they had decided Harry had to go, and if possible, Anna and myself as well. Probably

149

in a well-timed car accident.

'Hold on!' I said, and braked.

Confusion behind was obvious, and there was a withdrawal as far as closeness of following was concerned when I pulled away again, the distance between us was more marked, and remained so.

'He might 'ave bloody rammed you!' Harry said, sharply.

'Not when it belongs to a hospital,' I said. 'Mashed up front ends don't appeal to the customers. The image is bad.'

'You mean they won't smash us up?' said Anna.

'I don't know what they're trying to do,' I said. 'But certainly they'll hang on behind till we stop, and then what happens is up to the police.'

'If yer bloody get there,' said Harry, morosely, I thought. 'They don't think you're goen there no more do I. I'm not thinken police is right for this. What about Misses? I'm thinken for er!'

'I'm thinking Mrs Browne needs police more she needs doctors,' I said sharply.

'She won't get 'er money if you go to the police!' Anna wailed.

I said nothing but concentrated on driving as well as I could to keep the other car behind me. If once it got in front I felt the battle would be lost.

The lane suddenly turned and joined the main road alongside the pub. There were then a few cars in the pub car park at the front of the building. As I should have to slow right down to get round the right angle into the road, I turned instead into the car park, screamed round the parked vehicles and sped out on to the road on the other side of them. Behind me I heard a crash.

'E ave it a bloody car! Good, good!' Anna cried. 'I ope they are all dead!'

'Ere they come!' said Harry, in fatalistic tones. 'They looks funny at the front though. Bits angin off. And a geezer's chasen out the pub yellen somethen terrible. E aves a shotgun—Bang! E've shot at em! That's it, man. Give en tother barrel now—bang!'

In the mirror I could see only that the car had slewed round in the car park as if it was no longer sure where it was going. The commentary in this kind of peculiar English was, however, brilliantly explicit.

Then, as I got right into the main road I caught sight of the car squarely hitting one of the bollards which supported chains and formed the boundary of the car park. The bollard did not fall down, and the car seemed to stop.

We went on, but as we had had no time to choose we were going the wrong way along the road, back to Cob.

'That's fixed 'em!' Harry said, staring back. 'Steam up like a kettle it is. I reckon e've bust the bloody rad. That's what.'

That we were, from the heat of instant action, going the wrong way was just another feature of my exploits at Cob Weary. From the start I had never gone the right way.

A light came up on the dashboard.

'I must get petrol,' I said. 'Where's the nearest?'

'You're on the wrong road,' Harry said. 'But I got lots at Cob. Best get that afore they get orff that post, not that they could drive that wagon now.'

That warning light was not reliable. I had been caught by it before. Cob was then a half mile off. I thought we had better get that supply than be stranded altogether.

The road wasn't busy; most traffic seemed to go some other way, which probably was why it had no filling station.

We turned into the lane and the yard. As I stopped so did the engine, and all the warning lights came on. I switched off.

'Dry,' I said, getting out. 'Where's your supply?'

'I'll get it,' Harry said, and got out.

Anna, never to be left anywhere by herself, also got out.

'Misses! Arethusa!' she cried suddenly, and pointed to the open kitchen door.

Inside we could see the big woman sitting at the table, her head in her hands. Anna ran to her. I went towards the door and looked round as Harry came round the corner of the house carrying two jerrycans.

'Mrs Browne's back,' I said.

He dropped the cans and started to run. I went into the kitchen behind Anna. Harry stopped in the doorway, breathing heavily from running or emotion.

'What happened? Ow you got back?' Anna said, putting her arm round the woman's shoulders.

Mrs Browne lifted her head. She seemed half asleep.

'They would kill me, Anna. They tried upstairs, but when I woke just now I knew where I was. I knew where I was! I knew!'

'How you get ere?'

'There was a taxi outside. Abel's taxi from the village. I saw it and got out the window. Abel saw me. He did. He stopped as he was going. He helped me, Anna. Abel. We must pay him. I got out when I saw his car. I got out of the room by the window. They would kill me, Anna. I must go away from here too.' She began to cry.

'Yes, yes, we go away. We go away now. Right now. Arry, put the bloody gas in. Quick!'

Harry turned and went about the task of filling the car. He filled a few puddles on the ground as well, but most of the petrol went

153

into the tank.

'We must get right away, very, very quickly,' I said. 'They'll have to come and get her back, and we're all back here together. If they turn up now they'll catch us all—'

There was no need to finish, for even as I spoke, Harry shouted. I turned and the well-remembered gate-jammer slid into position and jammed the damned gate wall again. Two men got out.

Harry looked very angry.

'Hold it, Harry!' I shouted. 'He's got a gun.'

I remembered that shotgun as well as I remembered the car.

Harry held back, but I think it was because he had done business with these men and still was not sure of their intentions. At least, that was what it looked like to me.

I stood in the doorway facing the newcomers. Mrs Browne with Anna defending her, sat on at the table, too weary to do anything but just sit and let things happen. Which was probably what she had done all along.

The man with the gun, Wesson, looked as if he might be a doctor because he had a small leather bag in his hand.

'Where is Mrs Browne?' he said.

We seemed to be well stuck in a mud pond this time, so I threw a verbal grenade into the proceedings.

'She's inside, talking to her husband!' I said.

The doctor stiffened. The gunman jerked his head towards me and stared. The doctor recovered first, but I knew I had scored a bull.

'Her husband is dead,' the doctor said.

'The husband is pretending to be dead. In fact he is still in this racket with you.'

'You had better be careful what you say, Mr Keyes.'

'You know me?'

'Mrs Browne made a complaint about you interfering in her affairs.'

'Mrs Browne is now very pleased that I did.'

'I think you are making a mistake,' the doctor said coolly.

'I never make mistakes when men are pointing guns at me,' I said. 'And what is there to be mistaken about? You are working an undercover racket for disposing of dead bodies without trace, and Mrs Browne has been forced, by her not-so-dead husband, to take a small part in the transport of these cadavers.'

'Wait a minute!' Harry shouted. 'Bodies? What bodies?'

'The bodies in those boxes you collected,' I said.

'Shut up, you!' said Wesson, pointing the gun at Harry. 'This is wasting time, Doc. We must get her out. She's in danger if she doesn't have that treatment.'

'Have you any evidence to support this lunatic story?' the doctor said, staring at me.

'Yes, a lot. I have given it to the solicitors

this morning. It wasn't so difficult to link the evidence together once I had identified your nursing home.'

I was playing some wild guesses then, but what astonished me was that they seemed to be dead right.

The doctor decided to laugh.

'Where does one obtain all these corpses?'

'Well, you know, for some time past there has been heavy smuggling of illegal immigrants in container lorries, ordinary lorries, secret compartments in lorries and airless places in lorries. It was once guessed that about ten per cent did not survive being shut up so long. And of course, this is no loss to the transporter, who gets his few thousand dollars at the start of the operation. If the immigrant happens to die before he can reach a safe place, then disposal is essential. There are also people who pay for the accidental disposal of elderly relatives. Have you heard of that, Doctor?'

'I have heard of criminal libel, Mr Keyes,' said.

'It might expedite the matter if you started proceedings, Doctor,' I said.

I was being very clever, but whatever chances there had been of getting away alive were being lessened word by word. Being in the right only creates angry opposition, I have found.

Harry was standing in such a tense way that I fancied I would soon see the steam of fury and frustration begin to hiss from his ears.

The two women stayed so quiet behind us that I didn't even know if they were still there.

The doctor took a step towards me.

'We have come for Mrs Browne,' he said. 'And we will get her. Wesson!' He signalled the man to go forward with the gun.

But at that moment, a van drew up in the lane right behind the jamming car. It was loudly marked, 'Amy Robsart, Fishmonger, Kingston-on-Thames.'

A woman got out, the big, powerful woman I had last seen serving in the fried fish shop in Kingston. She came past the end of the hospital car and looked at Wesson grimly, then saw Harry.

'I wants er!' Amy Robsart said. 'I wants me rent!'

'Keep back!' Wesson said, laying the gun across the woman's belly.

I think it must have been a nervous reaction to unexpected interference coming just when Wesson was strung up to make his assault on our citadel. It was the wrong reaction to present to Amy Robsart.

I had never seen such a thing happen before, but the powerful woman flung her left arm out with a bunched fist at the end and with a back-hand swing, hit Wesson right across the jaw with such swinging force that he staggered back, dropped the gun, fell heavily against the car and knocked himself out.

The minute the gun was on the ground, Harry took a stride forward, picked up the doctor and lumped him against the open barn door, holding him there with a strong forearm across his throat.

'Wot the 'ell's goin' on 'ere?' Mrs Robsart demanded.

'You've just saved us from an armed gang,' I said, going away from the kitchen door. 'Don't worry about your rent. I'll guarantee that when we get rid of these villains.'

'Do you mean 'e would 'er shot that gun?' Mrs Robsart said, staring at me.

'Yes.'

'Stone me!' she said. 'I thought you was all arsin' about. Gawd! What did I do?' Then she started to laugh.

I picked up the gun. It was loaded in both barrels. For a moment I felt a weakening at the knees. After all the two men were in the corpse business and my body was as good as anybody's.

Harry brought the doctor to me by his hair. It looked like a final insult and gave the man much pain.

'What to do with 'im?' said Harry.

'Let him go,' I said. 'Keep Wesson as a witness. The doctor will do a moonlight in the hope of escaping the wrath to come. But tell the others, Doctor, before you disappear. They'll probably all disappear then.'

'Well, you're bloody generous, you are,' said

Mrs Robsart, staring. 'I wouldn't let them get away with it!'

'They won't get away with it,' I said. 'They're going home to a busted racket. Anyhow, we're keeping one of them. If you come inside a minute or two I'll give you a cheque.'

'But *you* don't owe me nothin',' she said.

'I represent Mrs Browne's solicitors,' I said. 'We pay for her.'

Mrs Robsart understood. When she came into the kitchen, Mrs Browne and Anna were not there. No doubt Anna had taken her away from possible danger.

'Do you think I'll be done for assault?' Mrs Robsart said, as she folded the cheque.

'He asaulted you by smacking you across the belly with a gun barrel, Mrs Robsart. Do remember that. You would never have swung your arm up in astonishment otherwise, would you?'

'You're not a bad firm, are yer? Might get in touch when I 'aves more trouble with these bloody planners. Dead agin shopkeepers they are.'

She went. The doctor's car was still there because it couldn't get out, but the doctor himself wasn't. Wesson still lay on the ground but only because Harry was standing by, looking down at him.

Letting the doctor, and therefore the rest of the gang, go free seemed to me the only thing to do if Mrs Browne was not to be rounded up

159

with them. I wanted to know more about just how much Mrs Browne had been pressured into doing what she did do. If the pressure had been slight and greed the supercharger, then she should be grouped with the others. But if not—Anyhow, I would leave all that to Miss Jansen and her partners.

The business of the dummy dead was undoubtedly a sort of cover for primitives like Harry, and perhaps others who might come into the house unexpectedly. It might even have been worked on me, and indeed the sight of that apparent Death Room had shocked me to the roots. But if one had seen a dead body, or heard about them being somewhere about this place, then realistic dummies could have covered up well, and perhaps they had done for some time. 'Body? What body? Ha, ha! That's an anatomical specimen!'

'Let him go, Harry,' I said.

'Wot?' said Harry, angrily.

'Let him go and give him a parting shot over his head to help him on his way.'

'O—kay,' said Harry, and hauled him up.

He was about to shove Wesson past the jamming car when a thought struck him.

'What about the car, then?'

'Let them ask the police for it,' I said. 'They can accuse you of holding it and ask the police to get it back—if they dare.'

Harry grinned then shoved Wesson out into the lane. Wesson was a fit man and he ran.

Harry waited to give him time, and then the silly arse shot him in the backside.

'It slipped,' Harry said. "'E's falled in the ditch now. Oh dear!' He grinned again, and went to help his fallen enemy, probably by pushing him deeper into the ditch.

I didn't look, but got in the nursing home car and shifted it into the farmyard so I could get mine out. That done, I went back into the house.

Anna and Mrs Browne were sitting in the big room. The woman had a glass in her hand and looked better.

'You'd better get out of here for a few days while things get sorted out,' I said. 'Have you got money?'

'Yes, yes. Will they come back?'

'You might know that.'

She shook her head. 'I don't.'

I watched her for a moment.

'Who tried to murder you?'

'Wesson. I think he heard somebody trying to get into the room. I'm not sure.'

'Probably me,' I said. 'I was trying to open a cupboard.'

'Will the police come?'

'I don't know,' I said. 'But I expect they will.'

'He held a pillow on my face—' She stopped there for a few seconds. 'I struggled to come up—for air, but I don't think he was there then—' She looked pretty bad.

'Forget all that stuff. It is all right now,'

Anna said.

I wrote down the name of a small hotel I know in Putney, gave Anna instructions how to get there, and told her to use the hospital car. I was sure the owners would ask the police where it was.

*   *   *

I made my separate way back to London and to Miss Jansen. She was pleased to see me. I told her all I had to tell of that day's events and she gave me news.

'The reason you went to Cob Weary in the first place is now no more. We doubted that Greco-Browne was really dead and that, therefore, there was some fiddle over the will. Both these reasons have now disappeared. Greco-Browne wasn't dead when you went down there, but he is now.'

She watched me with some amusement.

'Nothing to do with me, was it?' I said, quickly.

'Not really. But when the car following you hit the iron post Greco-Browne cricked his neck so badly he broke it and expired on the spot.'

'How sad,' I said. 'And what about the widow?'

'Well, her case will have to be handed to the police. They must prosecute, and her future depends on a good defence.'

'That's your pigeon,' I said.

*   *   *

When I pulled up in the mews by my house the hospital car was parked outside. I sat for a minute or so, looking at it, then I got out, opened my door with the key and shouted.

'Anna! Go home!'

The lady who got up from a chair with her back to me was my wife. She smiled.

'Hallo, darling!' she said. 'This is a surprise, isn't it?'

I kissed her and looked over her shoulder but saw no Anna.

'And guess what!' my wife said, beaming. 'I've got a maid at last! Sheer luck. She called just now and said she had heard I needed a maid at the little hotel of Jenny's in Putney, so there you are! Isn't that lucky?'

'Well, well,' I said, but to me it sounded like an apprehensive groan.